Time to go. Now!

Radley grabbed Honor's arm. "It's me," he said, whispering the words because the guard had appeared again, sprinting to the back of the camper, his radio buzzing with activity.

Out of sight. Armed. Dangerous.

Backup coming, and Radley didn't have time to ease into his escape plans or be gentle in his approach.

"Radley?" Honor whispered.

"Yeah," he responded. "Let's get out of here."

She nodded.

"Are you okay?" he asked.

"Fine," she murmured, her voice weak.

She was lying, because she had no choice but to be okay.

"I managed to get his gun," she said. "It's in your duffel. So, at least we're not unarmed. Let's go."

She stepped deeper into the trees, moving nearly silently, the shadowy forest embracing her.

He followed, because they had to put distance between themselves and the enemy.

They had to get to a town, find a phone, call for backup.

And once Honor was safe, once she'd been transported back to Boston, he'd return. Because there was no way he was going to let Absalom keep whatever dirty secrets he was hiding.

Aside from her faith and her family, there's not much **Shirlee McCoy** enjoys more than a good book! When she's not teaching or chauffeuring her five kids, she can usually be found plotting her next Love Inspired Suspense story or wandering around the beautiful Inland Northwest in search of inspiration. Shirlee loves to hear from readers. If you have time, drop her a line at shirlee@shirleemccoy.com.

Books by Shirlee McCoy

Love Inspired Suspense

FBI: Special Crimes Unit

Night Stalker
Gone
Dangerous Sanctuary

Mission: Rescue

Protective Instincts
Her Christmas Guardian
Exit Strategy
Deadly Christmas Secrets
Mystery Child
The Christmas Target
Mistaken Identity
Christmas on the Run

Classified K-9 Unit

Bodyguard

Rookie K-9 Unit

Secrets and Lies

Visit the Author Profile page at Harlequin.com for more titles.

DANGEROUS SANCTUARY

SHIRLEE MCCOY

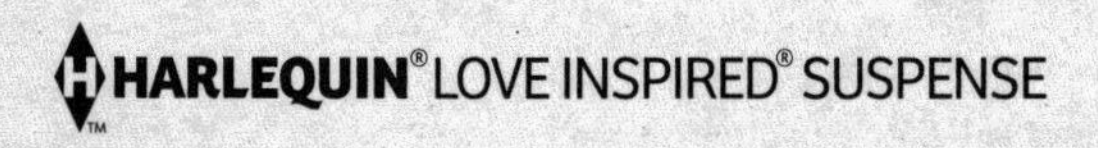

LOVE INSPIRED BOOKS

Recycling programs for this product may not exist in your area.

ISBN-13: 978-1-335-67882-9

Dangerous Sanctuary

This edition published by arrangement with Love Inspired Books.

www.Harlequin.com

Printed in U.S.A.

For all the law is fulfilled in one word, even in this;
Thou shalt love thy neighbour as thyself.

—*Galatians* 5:14

For you, because you picked up this book
and opened it to this page and read words
written from my heart to yours.

ONE

"Honor?"

A man's voice carried through the blackness that surrounded Honor Remington, reaching into a darkness so profound she wasn't sure how she'd drag herself out of it.

I need help. She tried to respond, but the words were trapped in her mind, stuck fast and unspoken.

Someone touched her shoulder, and she flinched, trying to open her eyes and look into the speaker's face.

Her lids felt glued together, her body sluggish and numb.

"Come on, Honor. You can do better than that," the man prodded, and something about his voice freed her.

Her eyes flew open, and she was looking into a familiar face. One she knew she should recognize: dark hair, hard-edged jaw and a scar at the corner of his mouth.

"There you go," he said, a note of relief in his voice.

"Who are you?" she asked, because she couldn't quite grasp the information. She knew him, and that was all she was certain of.

"You don't know?"

"Would I have asked if I did?" She tried to push herself into a sitting position, but her hands ached and burned, her body was weak and she collapsed again, falling back onto what felt like a thin pallet lying on an uneven floor.

"I'm Radley Tumberg," he replied. "We work together. FBI. Special Crimes Unit."

"I work for the FBI?" she asked.

"Yes." He leaned close, staring into her eyes, candlelight flickering across his face and shimmering in his hair. "And, I'm concerned that you don't seem to remember."

He rested a hand against her forehead, his skin rough and cool against her burning flesh.

She wanted to close her eyes and lie there with his cool palm against her hot forehead, but something was very wrong. Not just with her memory.

She glanced at the grayish interior of a round room, candlelight dancing on what looked like clay walls, a window opened out into a blue-black night.

"Where am I?" she asked. "What am I doing here?"

"This is Sunrise Spiritual Sanctuary," Radley replied. "You came here to find a friend."

"What friend?" It was a question she should have been able to answer herself. The fact that she couldn't would have brought her to full-out panic if she'd had the energy for it.

Instead, sluggish anxiety pulsed through her blood, and she pushed herself up again.

This time, she managed to sit, the cottony fabric of a pajama-like outfit sticking to her sweaty skin. A loose tunic top and elastic waistband-pants, they were clothes she'd have never purchased for herself.

She knew that.

Just like she knew she didn't belong in this place.

Now she just had to remember everything else.

"I don't have a name. All I have is the information you gave Wren, and it's minimal," Radley replied.

"Wren?"

"Santino. She's our supervisor. Which you might have an easier time remembering if your brain weren't being fried by fever." He touched her forehead again and dug into a duffle bag that lay on the floor nearby, pulling out a small bottle and tapping two pills into his hand. He held them out to her.

"What are they?"

"Acetaminophen. To bring the fever down."

"Oh." She reached for the pills, but her hands were wrapped in thick bandages, her fingers just peeking out from the ends of the gauze. "What happened to my hands?"

"I was wondering the same." He gently turned her hand so it was palm up, dropped the pills onto the gauze and grabbed a pitcher that sat on a small table near the window. There was a cup next to it, and he filled it, pressing it into her other hand. "Go ahead and take them. The sooner your fever goes down, the happier I'll be."

She nodded.

They had the same goal. Clear her thinking. Get her mind working again. She swallowed the pills and handed the cup back, searching the candlelit interior of the room for something that would tell her the story she'd forgotten.

A friend?

A sanctuary?

Her hands?

"Honor? You still with me? You'd better be, because if I don't get you out of here in one piece, Wren is going to have my head," Radley said.

Wren.

This time, the name set off a firestorm in her brain: a million images and memories and thoughts that were suddenly vying for her attention.

Because, of course, she was a special agent with the FBI. Computer forensic expert. High school nerd and all-around misfit.

And, he was Radley Tumberg—coworker, tough guy and all-around hero.

And Wren Santino was their supervisor.

She hadn't wanted Honor to come here. She'd tried to talk her out of it. She'd told her there'd be trouble, and that it was best to go through proper channels and allow the local authorities to do their jobs.

She'd been right.

Wren usually was.

It would have been helpful if Honor had remembered that *before* she'd decided to ignore her supervisor's warning.

But she hadn't.

She'd gone ahead with her plan, and now she was here, Radley eyeing her as if he thought she might fall apart.

"Sunrise Spiritual Sanctuary—a soothing retreat from a hectic and fast-paced life. Reboot. Renew. Rebuild. From the inside out," she quoted the pamphlet she'd been sent when she'd contacted the organization, because she could remember that, too.

Radley smiled again. "Your memory must be back if you're quoting propaganda material to me." He took another medicine bottle from his duffle and tapped a pill into her hand. "Take that."

"What is it?"

"An antibiotic. I got it from the agency doctor. Just in case."

"Typical you. Always prepared." She took the water he offered, chugging it down with the pill. Candlelight skipped in her periphery, the yurt spun, water sloshing from the cup and onto the bandages that covered her hands.

"It's okay," Radley said, his breath ruffling the hair near her ear, and she realized that, somehow, she was in his arms, being supported as he helped her lie down again.

"Lying down isn't on my agenda," she muttered, but she lay on the pallet anyway, waiting while the world stopped spinning.

"Of course, it's not. You're always moving. Unless you're hunched over a computer investigating," he responded.

"I'm not sure how you know that, since you're always on the move, too. Working cases outside the office," she replied, and he smiled.

"Your memory really is returning. What's

your friend's name and where can I find her? I want to get both of you out of here quickly. I have a bad feeling about this place."

"Mary Alice Stevenson. She's at a training seminar. Working toward a leadership position in this insane community."

"So, she's not here?"

"Not since I've been here. At least, that's what I've been told."

"You don't believe it?"

"You're not the only one who has a bad feeling about this place." The room had stopped spinning, and she was ready to go. She wanted out. She'd been wanting out since the moment she'd arrived and been escorted into the community, flanked by two men who were supposedly spiritual teachers but who'd acted like security guards.

She stood, legs shaky, hand reaching for something to steady herself.

She found Radley's arm, grabbing on before she remembered that would probably hurt. A lot.

It did, pain stabbing through her palm and up into her arm.

"You need to lie down again, Honor," Radley said, wrapping his arm around her waist and trying to urge her back down.

"I need to get out of here." She frowned.

"Is this still part of The Sanctuary? It's sure not the cushy cabin I was staying in when I arrived."

She'd paid her entire vacation savings to book a cabin at The Sanctuary, because she'd been determined to find Mary Alice. Deep soaking tub, fireplace, twin bed with a down mattress and cotton sheets. Handcrafted soaps and candles. Incense. Fresh flowers.

She'd been living the high life at the posh retreat meant to attract the wealthiest of seekers.

Of which, she was not.

But Mary Alice had certainly been. Wealthy and seeking.

Apparently, she'd found what she was looking for. If Honor had been given the chance to talk to her, she might have been able to make sense of that. She hadn't.

She'd done yoga beneath the stars and meditation in forest clearings. She'd engaged in philosophical conversations around campfires. She'd taken classes meant to awaken her to her deeper self, sitting through long days in closed classrooms in the meeting house.

She'd watched members of the community dressed in their cotton pajamas, clearing brush from the edges of the property, working in the greenhouse and in the kitchen, cleaning cabins for wealthy guests. Prepping and constantly busy.

But she hadn't seen Mary Alice.

She hadn't spoken to her.

And she needed to.

A biochemist who worked for a pharmaceutical company in Boston, Mary Alice loved urban sprawl and noise and people.

But, for some reason, she'd come here. She hadn't told Honor about her plans. She'd left without a phone call or a goodbye. Twenty years of friendship deserved more than that, and Honor would like an explanation.

She suspected she knew what it would be. Or, at least, part of it.

Mary Alice hadn't been herself since she'd called off her New Year's Eve wedding two nights before the big event. A year of planning, thousands of dollars, all of it tossed away after Mary Alice found out her fiancé, Scott, had cheated on her.

Good riddance. That had been Honor's thought, but Mary Alice had been heartbroken, embarrassed, lonely. All the things that might have made her easy pickings for a place like this one. A place that seemed like the perfect sanctuary from a hectic world but…

What?

There was something nagging at the back of

Honor's mind, some memory that might have given her a clue as to what had happened, how she'd ended up in a yurt, her hands bandaged, her thoughts muddled. The more she tried to grasp it, the more elusive it became.

Frustrated, she walked to a curved doorway and pulled back a heavy curtain that hung in the threshold. Cool air wafted across her skin, skipping along her hot cheeks and clearing her mind a little more.

She should remember this place. The yurt. The clearing it was sitting in. The grassy expanses that led to tall trees and thick forest.

"How long have I been here?" she asked.

"Two weeks."

"I can only remember maybe a week of that."

"You've been sick. At least, that's what they told me when I checked into this place," he responded.

"Sick? Injured is more like it."

"They failed to mention that part."

"There's a lot of things these people don't mention. Like the fact that leaving is a lot harder than entering."

"You tried to leave?"

"Sure. Once I knew that Mary Alice wasn't around, I had no reason to stay." She frowned. Whatever had happened to her, it had occurred after she'd asked to have her car keys, laptop and cell phone returned so that she could go home.

They'd all been taken when she'd arrived. Anything that would distract from the peaceful aura The Sanctuary provided had to be handed over during check-in. That had all been outlined in the literature she'd been sent. She'd played by the rules, because she'd wanted to see Mary Alice, talk to her, figure out how to get her to return home.

"So, you tried to leave, and then that happened?" He gestured to her hands.

"I remember asking for my belongings to be returned. Then, nothing."

"Like I said, I have a bad feeling about his place," he muttered.

"So let's get out of here." She stepped outside, and he grabbed her arm, pulling her back into the yurt.

"We're in the-middle-of-nowhere Vermont. No nearby community. No cell service. No weapons. My car keys and cell phone were confiscated at the gate, and I'm pretty certain they made sure they took yours."

"They did," she responded.

"So, how about we come up with a plan before we let anyone who's watching know that you're awake, lucid and ready to leave?"

She wanted to argue, because she didn't want to spend another second in The Sanctuary. It gave her the creeps, and there weren't a whole lot of things that did that.

But, without a vehicle, it would take a day to reach town.

"This is a great setup for holding people hostage and manipulating them," she said.

"I'd think you'd have clued into that before you arrived," he replied.

"Why do you say that?"

"The lack of web information. This place has no real online presence."

"I noticed that." The one-page website gave a brief description of The Sanctuary and provided a phone number. That was it. No reviews that she could find. No Facebook or Instagram or Twitter presence. "But what I was most concerned about was the fact that they'd somehow found Mary Alice, convinced her to come to their retreat and then brainwashed her into staying."

"Are you sure she didn't find them?"

"I'm not sure of anything. But I know that a place like this is as far outside her comfort zone as the big city is mine."

"You live in Boston," he reminded her. As if she might have lost that memory, too.

"During the week. I spend the weekend with

Dotty on the old family farm. She's going to be worried sick." Her mind rushed backward as she tried to remember the last time she'd been able to contact her grandmother.

"Dotty?"

"My grandmother. She's got to be worried out of her mind. I promised I'd contact her once a week. I don't think I've spoken to her since I left Boston."

"We'll get out of here, and then you can set her mind at ease." He had a calmness about him, a confident way of doing things that made people comfortable.

She'd noticed that the first time they'd met.

Right now, though, she wasn't in the mood for calm.

She was in the mood for action.

"We need to get to the meeting house. There are some locked offices there, and I'm sure that's where they're keeping our belongings," she said, stepping outside again.

Her gut was screaming that they needed to leave. Now!

And she always listened to her gut.

God whispering to her soul was how Dotty described it. Honor had no reason to call it anything else. She knew God worked in His own way and in His own time, but she also knew He always worked. He never slept. He had no limitations on His ability to see the past, the present, the future.

And Honor? She was fallible and flawed, prone to act first and regret later.

Which was how she always got herself into situations like this one.

"I'm going to work on that," she whispered.

"Good idea," Radley replied, his voice just as quiet as hers had been. He'd grabbed his duffle and followed her outside, moving silently beside her as she stepped further into the clearing.

"You can explain what you're going to work on after we talk to our friends," he continued, suddenly sliding his arm around her waist.

She tensed.

She didn't like people in her space, and he'd never seemed like the kind of guy who pushed himself in where he wasn't wanted.

"Friends?" she asked, suddenly aware of Radley's tension, of the clipped cadence of his voice.

"We'll talk later, honey," he replied, the endearment so surprising she almost missed the subtle nudge of his arm against hers.

But, she looked into his face, saw a warning in his eyes.

He leaned close, his lips nearly touching her

ear as he whispered, "The only way I could get in here was by pretending to be your husband."

"My hus—"

"You're beautiful in the moonlight, Honor," he cut in. "Have I ever told you that before?"

"Probably. But, feel free to repeat it every night for the rest of our lives," she said as several figures stepped from the shadows of some nearby trees.

Three. No four men. Tall. Moving quietly. Carrying machetes. Dressed, of course, in the light blue cotton uniform The Sanctuary's residents wore.

Radley had obviously known they were there.

He was on his game.

Honor was not.

That worried her, but she didn't have time to dwell on it.

"Hello, brother and sister," one of the men said. Tall and gangly, his dark hair pulled back in a man-bun, he was the leader of the group and called himself Absalom Winslow. Full-time residents of The Sanctuary called him Teacher.

Honor called him a charlatan. Not that anyone had asked.

"Honor," he said as he approached. "It's

good to see you awake. I'm sure you're happy to have your visitor with you."

Radley's grip on her waist tightened almost imperceptibly.

A warning, and she wasn't about to ignore it.

He'd provided a backstory. He'd given them information that had allowed him access to a closed and closely guarded compound. They hadn't had time to discuss it. She had no idea what he'd said.

She feigned weakness, her head resting against his solid bicep, and, for once, kept her big mouth shut.

Honor was smart. She was quick. And, for once, she was being quiet.

Radley didn't have time to be impressed.

Absalom Winslow was waiting for a response, his hired thugs staring at Radley as if they'd like to take him down with a few quick swipes of their machetes.

As long as they had no idea that the paperwork Radley had presented at the gatehouse was fake, things should be okay. For at least long enough to come up with a plan. One that did not include leaving The Sanctuary without his truck, his phone or Honor.

She was leaning against his arm, head pressed to his bicep. Something about that, about the thinness of her waist beneath his hand, the narrow width of her back, made his protective instincts kick in. That surprised him. He'd never viewed Honor as anything less than capable of taking care of herself and everyone around her. She might spend most of her time at the office working on computer systems and chasing rabbit trails through the World Wide Web, but she was smart, tough and capable.

Now she'd been weakened, diminished somehow by her stay at Sunrise Spiritual Sanctuary. It might have been a while since he'd been to church, but he knew faith never harmed or hurt.

From the looks of things this *spiritual* haven was doing both.

He eyed Absalom—gaunt cheeks nearly covered by thick facial hair. Dark eyes that glittered with zeal, or from drugs. Probably the latter. He'd been the one to approve Radley's entrance into the community. If there'd been any other recourse, he'd have refused.

"Honor? Are you pleased to have a visitor?" Absalom pressed, his gaze focused on Honor.

"You understated my wife's condition, Mr. Winslow. She's too weak to answer a lot of questions," he said.

Honor stiffened at the word wife, but continued her silence.

"Call me Absalom or Teacher. As my friends do."

"We're not friends. As I told you at the gate, I'm here to bring my wife home."

"The best thing for a struggling couple is to have time alone with one another. What better place to do that than here?"

"Currently, I'm thinking the hospital," he responded, taking a step forward, his arm still around Honor's waist.

"There's no need for a hospital. As I expressed to you when you arrived so unexpectedly, we've had a doctor visit Honor several times, and he's assured us that she's on the road to recovery."

"Burning with fever is not the road to recovery. I'd like an explanation for what happened to her. You're welcome to have your attorney contact me with the details, because we're not staying." He stepped past Absalom, his shoulder bumping one of the pajama-clad henchmen.

"Better watch your step, brother," the man growled, raising the machete slightly.

"Ditto," he replied, the hair on the back of his neck standing on end, his nerves alive with adrenaline.

These guys were well-trained paramilitary. Thick-muscled necks and shoulders. Upright stance. Buzz cuts. They moved in sync, turning as Absalom did, flanking him on either side as he fell into step beside Radley. Well-trained guards, and unless Radley was mistaken, they were carrying firearms beneath their flowy tunic-tops.

"Let's not be worldly in our approach to one another," Absalom said. "We must approach each other on the spiritual plane. With love and acceptance. Here is what I propose, Radley," he said. "You and Honor can stay in our luxury suite for the night."

"We're leaving."

"You're an attorney, Radley," Absalom said, because that was the cover Wren had suggested Radley use. Estranged husband. Attorney. Wealthy. "A man of logic and sound reasoning, I'd assume."

"A man with many connections in the outside world." Honor jumped into the conversation, catching on quickly. Just like she always did.

"If I didn't know your heart, Honor," Absalom murmured, "I would think that was a threat."

"Why would I want to threaten you?" she asked, her voice dripping with sarcasm.

Radley nudged her, hoping to reel her in before she enraged Absalom.

"That's a good question. We have been nothing but kind to you, providing for all your spiritual and physical needs."

"Right," she responded, and Radley nudged her again.

"And now, your *husband* is here. You've been estranged for a season, and it is not the will of the universe or nature that a lifetime partnership should end."

"I don't think the universe cares about the state of our union," Radley replied.

There was something worrisome about the way Absalom had said *husband*. Just enough emphasis on the word to make Radley wonder what he knew and how he knew it. Wren had produced a fake marriage license, a phony business card. She'd even had an agency tech put together a website advertising Radley's nonexistent law office. The cover was solid, and there was no way it could be blown by a simple internet search.

"God is concerned about all His children," Absalom said. "And He has given me authority in this small part of the world to ensure that His will is done and that His concerns are the concerns of the community."

"Tell you what." Radley stopped walking, his arm slipping from Honor's waist. She'd straightened, was standing beside him—shoulder-height, swaying on her feet, but trying to look steady and ready to fight. "You go ahead and concern yourself with whatever you want. After you give me my keys and my cell phone."

"I'm sorry to say, that won't be happening tonight."

"If you'd rather me find the keys and phone myself, I can do that."

"That won't be happening either." Absalom nodded toward one of the guards.

"Come on. I'll take you to your new accommodations," the man said, grabbing Radley's arm.

"We're leaving," Radley asserted, shrugging away, his duffle falling to the ground.

Honor grabbed it, her face pale in the darkness, the bandages on her hands stark white.

The guard grabbed for him again, and Radley side-swiped his knee, not bothering to watch as he fell. He'd grown up fighting. He knew how it was done. Fast and dirty. But now he mixed the skills he'd been taught in the military with the street-smart thuggery he'd learned growing up in the inner city. The second guard fell as quickly as the first, and he was facing the third.

Only this guy had pulled a gun and was pointing it straight at Radley's heart.

"You're going to be sorry for that," he growled.

Radley kicked the gun from his hand. It skittered into the undergrowth nearby, and they both went for it. Radley reached it first, swinging it toward the other man.

"Stop," he commanded.

And the world stilled.

The night went silent.

For a moment, there was nothing but the two of them staring each other down.

And then Absalom spoke, his voice as cold as ice.

"These kinds of brawls are never in the will of the universe or God. Put the gun down."

Radley's gaze shifted from his potential attacker to Absalom.

He had Honor by the arm, a gun pressed to her cheek.

Radley had been a sniper in the military. He knew how to take a man out, but there were three other men getting to their feet. Two of them still armed, and he couldn't risk Honor's life. He had to trust, as his mother often said, that God would make things right in His own good time.

He set the gun down, raised his hands in the air and waited.

TWO

Honor didn't much like having a gun pressed to her cheek. She liked even less that she felt weak, her legs shaky. At her best, she could probably take Absalom down easily.

She was not at her best.

She wasn't even close to it.

Radley's gaze was focused on Absalom. "You are making a big mistake," he said.

"The mistake is yours. You've unbalanced the peace of the community. In God's kingdom, my word is law. A little time to think, and I'm sure you'll both agree," Absalom intoned, shoving the barrel of the gun a little deeper into Honor's flesh.

If that were his idea of peace, she'd like to know how he described war.

"Take Mr. Tumberg to the meditation room," he commanded. Then, he swung around, his grip still tight, the gun still pressed against her cheek.

The yurt was just a few yards away, candlelight shimmering on the ground below the window. A peaceful scene in any other setting, but right now, it was terrifying.

Behind her, there was a scuffle, fists against flesh, quiet grunts. She tried to turn her head, but the gun was pressed so tightly against her skin that she couldn't.

"Do you know the story of Lot's wife?" Absalom asked, his lips against her ear.

Her flesh crawled, all the heat that had been roaring through her body replaced by icy fear. "I'm familiar with it."

"Then you know that looking back didn't end well for her."

"I want to see my husband."

"I'm disappointed in you, Honor. I thought you were more in tune with the goals of the community."

"I came here to get away from things," she lied as she allowed herself to be marched to the yurt. Her legs still felt wobbly, but her mind was clearer, her thoughts crisp. "Not to join your community."

"Part of the experience offered at Sunrise Spiritual Sanctuary is tuning into the peacefulness of nature and of the universe. You've been fighting that since you arrived. That's why you've been ill."

"I think I've been ill because of whatever happened to my hands," she countered, keeping her voice low, because she didn't want any of his guards to join them.

Even weak, she might have a chance against Absalom.

She'd been trained to take down perps. As a computer forensic expert, she didn't have much of an opportunity to put that skill to use, but she kept up on technique, training hard and facing off against much larger and stronger opponents in the gym and on the sparring mat. Her job required it. Even if it hadn't, she'd have attended weekly self-defense classes. Just in case.

Life was full of surprises.

Some of them great.

Some of them not.

It was good to be prepared for either.

"The burns on your hands were healing nicely—"

"Burns?"

"You fell into the firing pit. Sister Hannah was showing you how to make pots. You don't remember?" he asked, the gun slipping away from her cheek.

She glanced back, saw Radley being manhandled away from the clearing and into the forest.

"No, but it seems like something I should remember."

"You tripped and fell. Fortunately, you were able to catch yourself with your hands. Otherwise, it would have been your face and body that were burned. We brought a doctor in immediately. He patched you up and gave you some medication to stave off infection. You should have improved rapidly, but you declined. Our health suffers when we're fighting the natural order of things."

"What is the natural order?" she asked.

"Peace and harmony with nature, with self and with others."

There were a million things she wanted to say, but she kept her mouth shut, afraid she'd get herself into more trouble if she opened it.

Right now, her focus needed to be on escaping and finding Radley.

"That sounds wonderful."

"Of course, it does. You're a kindhearted soul. A woman who takes care of her elderly grandmother and never complains about doing so."

"What do you know about my grandmother?"

she asked, her blood running cold. Dotty was getting older. She wasn't as strong as she'd once been. That made her vulnerable, and the thought of Absalom knowing anything about her made Honor's stomach churn.

"Only what you've mentioned to fellow guests," he replied, the gun shifting, his grip loosening as they reached the yurt door.

She might not remember everything that had happened since her arrival, but she knew she hadn't mentioned Dotty to anyone. Her private life was private. Even people at work didn't know much about what she did when she left the office at the end of every day.

"I don't recall mentioning my grandmother at all."

"Of course, you did. You love her, and you want what's best for her." He tucked the gun into a holster beneath his tunic and pulled a syringe from his pocket.

"What's that?" She took a step away, Radley's duffle thumping against her thigh. Whatever it was, she wanted nothing to do with it.

"The medicine the doctor prescribed for you. Your husband's arrival postponed your dose. We're a couple hours late, but I'm sure it won't matter." He smiled, his eyes empty and lifeless, candlelight dancing across his gaunt face.

"What kind of medicine?"

"An antibiotic."

"In that case, it won't be necessary. Radley gave me an oral antibiotic a few minutes ago."

"It's necessary, Honor. Everything that is happening is necessary for the good of the community and, of course, for you." He uncapped the syringe.

She didn't think. She reacted. Swinging the duffle at Absalom's legs, putting all her strength into it. He fell, the syringe dropping from his hand.

"You shouldn't have done that, Honor," he bellowed as he scrambled to retrieve it.

But she was there first, all the sluggishness gone in a wave of adrenaline that demanded action. She had the syringe, was plunging it into his shoulder, injecting him with whatever it contained. She had no idea what.

She couldn't care.

Not with Radley's life at stake.

Not with Mary Alice missing.

Not with Absalom knowing exactly what Honor's weakness was.

Dotty.

She'd do anything for the woman who'd raised her after her parents died.

She ran outside, cold air slapping her cheeks, her heart thudding crazily. She could still feel the fiery heat in her hands, but she was shivering with cold and terror.

Not for herself.

For the people she cared about.

She had to get Radley and get out. Find a phone. Call her uncle, Bennett. Make sure that Dotty was okay.

She ran across the clearing, heading for the woods where Radley had disappeared. No plan in mind except for getting to him.

It took seconds to realize there were no sounds of pursuit. Not feet pounding on the ground. No growled threats or shouted commands. No click of a gun safety. No bullet.

Nothing.

She glanced back, saw a pile of light fabric at the entrance to the yurt. No. Not fabric. Absalom.

She skidded to a stop at the tree line, gasping for breath, still frantic, but thinking clearly and more like herself than she'd been since Radley pulled her from darkness.

Absalom had a gun.

She had nothing.

If he were unconscious, it would be an easy thing to take his firearm. It would also be easy to go back into the yurt and grab Radley's duffel. They were at least twenty miles from the nearest town, tucked away in the middle of the

Vermont wilderness. From what she could remember, there weren't many residential properties nearby.

If they couldn't obtain a vehicle, they'd have to walk out.

If they had to walk, they'd need supplies and a weapon.

She watched Absalom for a minute, counting the seconds in her head and praying that she wasn't making a mistake. Time was always precious. She'd learned that the day her parents had been killed in a car accident. She'd been twelve. An only child who'd been given everything she'd needed and most of what she'd wanted.

She wouldn't call her younger self spoiled, but she'd had it good. Horseback riding lessons, dance, gymnastics, archery. She'd had a puppy, her own bedroom and parents who were devoted to helping her become her best self.

She'd been too young to appreciate it.

And then they were gone. Killed on the way to her mother's doctor's appointment.

Just like that.

And, at twelve years old, she'd learned just how valuable time was. She'd have given everything she owned to have more of it with her parents.

When Absalom didn't move, she walked

back to the yurt, approaching him cautiously. He was breathing, his shoulders rising and falling, his body limp.

"Absalom?" she said, staying just out of reach.

When he didn't respond, she crossed the distance between them, crouching next to him and touching his shoulder. The syringe was gone. He had to have pulled it out as he was running after her.

He was out, too. Not in distress. Just knocked out cold, his breathing heavy and deep, his pulse slow and steady.

She rolled him to his side, lifted the tunic and grabbed the gun, checking to see if it was loaded before backing away.

She walked into the yurt and grabbed the duffel, glanced around the room and spotted her backpack leaning against the wall. She hefted it onto her shoulders, the gauze on her hands unraveling. She removed it, wincing as it pulled away from raw skin.

Absalom had said she'd fallen into a firing pit and burned them.

She didn't remember, but the skin looked burned, opened blisters dried out and cracked.

She didn't have time to think about it. Eventually, Absalom's guards would be back. She and Radley needed to be far away from The Sanctuary before then.

The camper they'd tossed Radley into was boarded up, the interior pitch-black and filled with the scent of rotting wood and mold. He lay on his back, waiting for his eyes to adjust, his fingers working at the knotted rope that had been used to bind his wrists.

They'd been tied in front. That had been the guards' first mistake. The second was leaving him alone inside a camper that looked more like a crumbling tin can than a prison. He'd gotten a decent look as he'd approached, noting the position of the door and windows.

Muffled voices drifted through the thin walls, and he imagined the guards felt successful. They'd subdued him, bound him and imprisoned him. The scent of tobacco and nicotine drifted on the still, stale air. One or more guards smoking as Radley slowly worked free of the rope.

It took more time than he wanted it to, but he finally managed to loosen the rope. It slid from his wrists, and he sat. His eyes had adjusted enough to turn pitch-black darkness into dark gray shadows. There was a small table jutting out from one wall. No chairs. A double bed shoved up against the far end of the camper.

Moonlight gleamed through holes in the ceiling and walls. He moved silently, reaching for the rope that bound his ankles and untying it quickly. He shoved it and the rope that had been used on his wrists into his jacket pocket and stood.

The rotting floor gave a little, bowing as he walked to the door.

The murmur of voices had ceased, but the scent of cigarette smoke remained strong enough that he was certain at least one guard was outside. He could have gone on the offensive, kicked open the door and disarmed the man, but he'd rather his escape go unnoticed for as long as possible. He needed to get out of the camper and get back to Honor before anyone set off an alarm.

Whatever was happening in The Sanctuary could be determined after she was safe.

He walked to the bed, climbing onto the musty mattress and feeling for the edges of the plywood that covered a window just above it. It moved easily, and he pulled it down, revealing the open hole where glass had once been. Not a large opening, but he could squeeze through.

The guard was on the move, his footsteps audible—boots on packed earth and dry grass, fabric rustling. He seemed to be moving away rather than toward Radley's position. Bored and restless, maybe. Definitely not worried about his prisoner escaping.

Radley eased his shoulders through the window and lowered himself to the ground. The night had gone quiet again. He did the same, waiting and listening as the guard changed directions and moved toward him.

He ducked beneath the camper, shimmying on his belly, hands pressed into damp earth and decaying leaves. If the guard noticed the missing plywood and uncovered window, he'd have to be taken down. Minutes passed, the scent of cigarette smoke filling the air again. A shadow moved to his right, and he watched booted feet walk in the direction of the camper's door.

That was what he wanted and had been hoping for.

He shimmied out, ready to make his escape.

But something moved in his periphery—a shadow separating from the trees. There. Gone. There again. He watched as it approached, tried to determine whether it was a guard or Absalom.

It didn't occur to him until it was almost too late that the shadow could be Honor. That she might have escaped Absalom and be making her way to him.

He knew, of course, that she was tough.

Everyone who worked in the Special Crimes Unit was.

They saw the worst of the worst, the debased and the vile. Men and women who were as close to irredeemable as anyone could be. Dealing with people like that required sharp edges, keen intelligence and good training.

Honor had all those things.

But she worked on computers, spending most of her time in a chair, with her eyes on the screen. She followed electronic footprints and found her way in and out of the cyber world.

She did not fight her way out of danger, throw punches or disarm dangerous criminals. Maybe that was why he'd underestimated her resourcefulness and her willingness to attempt an escape.

Whatever the case, he wasn't expecting her, and he was ready to rush the shadow, slam it to the ground, subdue it. Start what could only turn into a fight for survival, because two against one weren't good odds. Especially when the two were armed.

But moonlight glinted off pale skin and light cotton, and he realized he *was* watching Honor approach. She moved like a sprite, darting here and there, trying to find a way into the clearing that wouldn't allow her to be seen.

He slipped through long grass, staying low

and moving as silently as he could, heading in her direction and trying to stay out of the guard's line of sight.

He couldn't call out to her.

He couldn't warn her that he was approaching.

He couldn't count on her not crying out when he suddenly appeared.

He slipped into the woods fifty feet away from her position. The fact that she didn't notice bothered him. If she were going to play cat and mouse, she needed to learn to play it well. She also needed to learn that it wasn't just the cat she needed to be concerned with. There were always larger, more aggressive predators, and it was smart to be on the lookout for them.

He glanced at the camper. The guard was on the move again, pacing in front of the door, lighting another cigarette and walking around the side of the structure.

Out of sight and maybe moving toward the back where the missing plywood would give away Radley's escape.

He was behind Honor in seconds.

She faced the clearing, his duffel at her feet, a backpack on her shoulders. She looked vulnerable, her hair a wild mass of flyaway strands, her body seemingly dwarfed by the pack she carried.

He didn't want to startle a scream out of her, didn't want a fight. He meant to whisper her name, let her know that he was there, but the guard sprinted around the side of the camper, radio out, yelling into it as he bounded up three steps that led to the door and kicked it open.

Time to go. Now!

Radley grabbed Honor's arm as she jumped back, apparently startled by the guard's behavior.

She was startled by his touch, as well.

She yanked away, grabbing the duffel and swinging it in his direction.

He caught it easily, pulling it from her hands.

"It's me," he said, but she didn't seem to hear. She was fighting all-out, swinging her fists and attempting a sideswipe to his knee that would have worked if he weren't as well-trained in self-defense as she was.

He grabbed her forearm and pulled her into his chest.

She struggled, but he was larger and stronger, one arm on hers, the other wrapped tightly around her waist. Not enough space between them for her to use hands or feet against him.

"It's me," he repeated, whispering the words in her ear because the guard had appeared again, sprinting to the back of the camper, his radio buzzing with activity.

Out of sight. Armed. Dangerous.

Backup coming, and Radley didn't have time to ease into his escape plans or to be gentle in his approach. "How about you stop fighting me, so we can get out of here while we can?"

"Radley?" she whispered, her breath hot through his shirt. She'd stopped struggling, seemed to finally understand who he was.

"Yeah," he responded.

She nodded, her head bumping his chest, her body suddenly limp.

"Are you okay?" he asked, his heart thundering with the need to get away, his mind screaming that they had to go while they still had the chance.

"Fine," she murmured, her voice weak.

She was lying, because she had no choice but to be okay.

She knew it.

He knew it.

If they were caught, if they were imprisoned again, it wouldn't be in a ramshackle camper. *If* they were imprisoned. The other option was burial in a shallow grave somewhere deep in the forest. By the time Wren realized they were both missing, it would be too late. Even the best-trained cadaver dogs would have difficulty finding remains in a wilderness of this size, and proof of any crime would be long gone.

"All right," he murmured against her hair, the scent of candle flames and rich earth filling his nose.

He told himself she wasn't a victim, reminded himself that she was a trained law enforcement officer, a special agent prepared for whatever came.

But she was trembling, and when she stepped away she swayed.

"Honor..." He didn't know what he would have said, what he could have said.

"I managed to get Absalom's gun." She cut off before he could finish. "It's in your duffel. So at least we're not unarmed. Let's go."

She stepped deeper into the trees, moving nearly silently, the shadowy forest embracing her.

He followed, because there was no other choice.

They had to put distance between themselves and the enemy.

They had to get to a town, find a phone, call for backup.

And once Honor was safe, once she'd been transported back to Boston, he'd return. Because there was no way he was going to let Absalom keep whatever dirty secrets he was hiding.

THREE

The thing about life, Honor had learned, was that sometimes you didn't get a choice in how it played out, but you always had a choice in how you responded to it.

After her parents had died, Uncle Bennett had become her legal guardian. Honor's mother had been an only child whose parents had moved to Florida a decade prior. Aside from Bennett, Honor's only other living relative had been Dotty. Her grandmother had lived on a five-hundred-acre farm that had been in her husband's family for generations. Ninety minutes outside of Boston, the property was far from the Boston suburb where Honor had been living with her parents.

Bennett had been single, childless and focused on building his career as a defense lawyer. Honor figured he'd probably agreed to be her guardian because he'd felt like he had no choice.

Whatever the case, he had agreed and, after her parents' deaths, he'd moved into their suburban house and done his best to shepherd Honor into adulthood.

But he'd been busy.

She'd been nearing her teen years.

They'd both tried, but it had been Dotty who'd held them together. Every weekend, Bennett had shipped Honor off to the farm. He'd done the same on holidays. Summers were always spent on the lush acreage, helping Dotty with the garden, mucking stalls and riding horses.

Honor had loved that.

She'd loved Dotty.

She and Bennett, on the other hand, had never been close. He'd often made it clear that he'd be happy when she was eighteen and they could go their separate ways.

She'd purposed not to let that change her. She'd studied hard, graduating from high school a year early and attending MIT on full scholarship. She'd worked full-time, attended classes full-time and maintained her GPA by skipping sleep and parties. There'd been no time for other things. Not hobbies. Not vacations.

Not relationships.

She'd tried a few times, dating men she

thought were as driven as she was. It always seemed that they asked too much, demanding time and attention she'd wanted to expend on other things.

And, now, she was nearing thirty. Alone.

Her best friend suddenly gone from her life.

She'd been telling herself for months that it was okay. That she would make the best of it the same way she'd made the best of other things in her life.

And, now, she was here: putting one foot in front of the other, trudging through thick forests without any plan beyond getting away.

She'd make it work.

She had to.

She just wasn't sure how.

Somewhere in the distance, people were charging through the woods, branches breaking, leaves crackling, voices calling. She and Radley moved silently. No discussion. No communication. Just heading away from the danger.

Hopefully, not into something worse than what they were leaving behind.

Vermont was a beautiful state, filled with gorgeous vistas, but the wilderness could be deadly. Getting lost out here could end just as badly as staying at The Sanctuary.

"We should probably have a plan," she murmured, keeping her voice low because sound carried, and she didn't want Absalom's thugs to hear.

"We do," Radley replied.

"Would you care to share it with me?"

"We keep heading south until we reach the road. Follow that to town. Unless we find a residential property before then. If we do, we'll try to borrow a phone."

"I'm glad one of us knows where the road is and which direction we need to go to find it."

"The moon has nearly set." He stopped, pulling her up so that they were arm to arm. "See it?"

She did. Now that he mentioned it. A yellow-white orb gleaming through the trees to their left.

"Yes."

"I'm using that as a guide."

"What are you going to use when it's set?" she asked, still not certain they were heading in the right direction.

"I'm hoping we'll hit the road before that happens."

"And if we don't?"

"We'll camp for the night and use the sun to guide us in the morning."

"I don't think camping out with Absalom's men on our trail is a good idea."

"You think getting lost is a better one?"

"What I think is that I should have stayed in Boston and let the local authorities locate Mary Alice. Just like Wren said."

"Why didn't you?" He started walking again, and she followed, picking her way through thick undergrowth, thorns catching at the gauzy cotton pajamas she wore.

"Because Mary Alice is my best friend, and I didn't want to wait for the slow wheels of justice to turn. Plus, I was worried. Disappearing like this is out of character for her."

"Do you have any idea why she did it?"

"She called off her wedding in December. Maybe that. Maybe something else. She wasn't talking much these past couple of months. Her parents gave me access to her computer. I looked at her search history, her email accounts. There was nothing there that hinted she was looking for a place like The Sanctuary."

"Cults have a way of finding vulnerable people."

"They usually don't prey on people like Mary Alice."

"What kind of person is she?"

"Successful. Has a loving family. A good network of friends."

"Wealthy?"

"Yes. But not vulnerable. Although..."

"What?"

"Like I said, she broke up with her fiancé right before the wedding. She'd found out he was cheating."

"Seems like that would make someone vulnerable."

"I should have realized that." And she regretted how easily she'd allowed herself to excuse the distance that had been growing between them, how eager she'd been to believe there was nothing wrong.

"It's not your fault," Radley said as if he could read her mind.

She didn't respond. She was tired, her hands throbbing, her legs heavy. She didn't have the energy for explanation or debate.

"How long do we walk before deciding the road is in some other direction?" she asked instead.

"You're tired."

"I'm worried about getting lost out here. If we're going the wrong direction, we're walking into hundreds of miles of wilderness."

"You're not putting much faith in my navigational abilities."

"Because I know nothing about them. Statistically speaking—"

"How about we don't?"

"What?"

"Talk statistics. Math was never my strong suit."

"What was?"

"Survival," he replied.

If he'd been any other guy she'd ever spent time with, she'd have laughed. But then, the guys she'd spent time with outside of work preferred the inside of computer labs to the great outdoors.

"I'm glad one of us has those skills."

He stopped, gave her time to move up beside him. "See that?"

He pointed through the trees.

For a moment, she thought she was seeing the moon again—a shiny ball low in the sky. Then she saw another of the same. And another.

"Lights," she breathed, stepping forward.

"Wait." He snagged her pack, pulling her to a stop. "Those are the gate lights."

"Gates?"

"To the compound? You remember arriving, right?"

"I arrived during the day. The lights were off," she responded. "The parking lot is right across from the gate."

"Right. Both our vehicles are there. I parked next to your Explorer."

"My Explorer isn't going to do either of us any good without keys."

"I have a spare key attached to the chassis of my truck."

"I'm surprised you'd keep a spare key in an easily accessible location. You don't seem like the kind of person who takes chances."

"I'm not, but for this trip, I decided an extra key might be a good thing."

She wasn't surprised.

She'd seen the way Radley prepared for work, the way he tackled cases, the way he pushed himself. She knew he didn't go into anything unprepared. And, going into a place like Sunrise Spiritual Sanctuary would make most law enforcement personnel worry.

A compound in the middle of nowhere.

Very little information about it.

Word of mouth bringing in clients.

Endless potential for things to go wrong.

Honor had known before she'd arrived that there was something more to Sunrise Spiritual Sanctuary than what was listed on their webpage. Instead of doing more research, maybe visiting the area and asking some questions, she'd contacted The Sanctuary and pushed ahead in her effort to find Mary Alice. She'd brushed aside her gut instincts. She'd brushed aside Wren's concerns. She'd even brushed aside Dotty's disappointment that they would miss their weekends together.

"Sometimes, my stubborn determination is a detriment to my well-being," she muttered.

"We can talk about that during the debriefing," Radley responded, and she thought she heard amusement in his voice. "Let's get to the truck and get out of here."

"Good idea," she agreed quickly.

She stepped forward. He pulled her back.

"Hold on."

"Why?"

"Listen."

The way he said it made her hair stand on end.

"What am I listening for?" she whispered.

"The silence."

Now that he mentioned it, things had gone quiet. No branches breaking. No muffled voices. No crickets chirping or animals rustling. No sign that they weren't the only two living beings in the vicinity.

Absalom's men had changed tactics. She didn't need to be a specialized field agent to realize that.

"They're probably heading to the parking

lot," she whispered, her head bent close to his, the words barely carrying through the darkness.

"That's what I'm thinking. I know part of the compound is fenced. I was able to do some reconnaissance before I checked in, but I don't know how far the fence line stretches. Do you?"

"No. But, I know it stretches at least two miles. I walked that far several times, trying to find its end. All I found was more fence."

"They've lost our trail, but they know we're going to try to escape the compound. They'll be expecting us to make a run for the gate or the parking lot. We'll take another route." He started walking, tugging her with him.

"You know the fence is seven feet, right?" she asked.

"Yes."

"I can barely climb a five-foot one."

"You can do anything you put your mind to," he replied.

"The idea of mind over matter? It's vastly overrated."

"How about we have that debate after we get out of here?"

"Is that your way of telling me to be quiet?"

"It's my way of telling you that you need to conserve energy. We have a seven-foot fence to climb."

No way was she going to be able to do that. Not with her hands burned and blistered, her body weak, a backpack filled with clothes on her back.

But pointing that out wasn't going to do any good, so she kept her mouth shut and let him lead her back into the woods.

It took money to build a seven-foot fence. It took a lot of it to build one that stretched as far as The Sanctuary's seemed to. Radley eyed the smooth wooden planks. Climbing them would be easy enough. He was six-foot-three and had climbed taller structures during military training. Even with help, though, Honor might struggle. She was a foot shorter than he was, weakened from illness and fever, hands blistered and raw. The surface of the fence was smooth. Free of hand or footholds.

An odd design. No crossbeams on the inside, so they had to be exterior. Not a good idea if the goal was to keep outsiders from climbing in.

But maybe the goal was to keep insiders from climbing out.

For Honor's sake, he'd have followed the length of the fence, looking for another exit or an end to the fencing, but they didn't have time. If Absalom's men had brains in their heads, they'd be guarding the gate *and* patrolling the fence line. Better to have her hands hurt a little more than to have her shot.

"We'll climb over here," he said, leading her from the thick woods and onto a three-foot-wide cleared swath of grass. None of the trees were close enough to the fence to be used as ladders or as leverage. He had to believe that was planned.

He wanted to know what was going on in The Sanctuary, what dark secrets Absalom was hiding. First, though, he wanted to get Honor to safety.

"The fence is taller than I remembered," she murmured.

"Not so tall we can't get over it," he responded, the hair on the back of his neck standing on end, his nerves alive with warning.

They were standing between the fence and the trees, exposed to anyone who might be looking for them, and he knew plenty of people were.

"Currently, anything would be too tall." Her teeth were chattering as if her fever were returning. "As a matter of fact, I'd say that fence is an impossible task."

"Nothing is impossible, Honor," he replied, reaching into his duffel and pulling out the handgun she'd told him was there.

"Diving to the deepest part of the ocean is," she responded, her voice barely a whisper in the darkness. "Digging a hole from North America to the other side of the globe is. Skating on thin ice, walking in wet grass while wearing stiletto heels."

"I get your point, but I'm not asking you to do any of those things." He didn't have a holster, so he checked the gun's safety and tucked it into the waistband of his jeans.

"Radley, we both know I'm slowing you down. You can get over that fence and get to help before I manage to take three steps."

"I never thought of you as the kind of person who'd exaggerate," he said.

"What kind of person did you think I was?"

"The kind of person who enjoys being accurate, logical and factual."

"I am."

"Good, then you know that's it's not going to take long for either of us to get over the fence." He eased the backpack from her shoulders and shrugged into it. "Come on. Let's go."

"Radley, I want you to go ahead. We both have a better chance of survival if you do."

"I'd have a better chance. You wouldn't. That wouldn't work for Wren. It doesn't work for me, and I'm sure it won't work for you."

"What works for me is both of us getting out

of here alive, so that I can find Mary Alice. That's not going to happen if we're standing here bickering while armed men are searching for us."

"Bickering?"

"Fighting. Arguing. Disagreeing."

"I know what it means, I'm just surprised to hear you use such an old-fashioned word."

"Old-fashioned? Dotty would take offense at that." She was watching him, her eyes gleaming in the darkness, her face a pale oval, her clothes nearly glowing in the darkness. A beacon drawing the eye of anyone searching for them.

"She says it a lot, huh?"

"She did. When I was young and arguing with my uncle about curfews and grades."

"Did she also use the words *grit*, *gutsy*, *daring*? Because that's what you're about to be. Let's go. Over the fence."

A dog howled, the sound ringing through the forest, and his pulse jumped, his heart racing. He knew the sound of a hunting dog. This one was close.

"Are there dogs here?" he asked.

"Yes. A couple of guard dogs that patrol the meeting hall at night and some hunting dogs that are used by the residents of the community." She nodded, her eyes wide, the pulse in the hollow of her throat jumping frantically.

"I wonder how good those dogs are at tracking escapees?" he muttered.

"We may be the first people who've have the need to escape, but the hunting dogs are bloodhounds. They have great noses."

"That's what I was afraid of. Come on. Let's go." He lifted her. She was slighter than he'd expected, her back narrow, her body light. He'd always thought of her as athletic and strong. She had a presence that demanded attention and seemed to fill every room she entered. Chatty, quick with smiles and compliments, she was the opposite of Radley. Except in her need for justice, her determination, her dogged focus when it came to solving a case or finding a criminal.

Now she seemed determined to pull herself over the fence. She'd grabbed the top and was struggling to drag her body over. He gave her legs a boost, holding on until she managed to scramble up and drop one leg over the top.

Behind him, the hound was crashing through trees, baying wildly.

Radley slung the duffel strap over his shoulder, grabbed the top of the fence and pulled himself up beside Honor. He'd climbed fences dozens of times. He'd run from danger even more times than that. He knew how to move quickly and quietly. But Honor was still perched on the fence like she was riding a horse. One leg to one side. One to the other. Hands clutching the wood. Backlit by the setting moon, pale skin, light hair, light-colored clothes. She was a sitting duck, an easy target.

"It's okay," he said, because he thought she was frozen in fear.

"I know, but I wasn't going to jump until you were out of there. Just in case."

"In case what?"

"You needed help," she replied, and then she threw her second leg over the fence and dropped to the ground.

FOUR

Honor dropped hard and fast, stumbling forward. Falling. She landed on her hands and knees, pain shooting through her palms and up her arms. She felt it in her shoulders, her jaw, her head.

If she'd had time, she'd have dropped to her stomach, lain in the cold grass, trying to catch her breath and get her bearings. But Radley dropped down beside her, reaching for her arm and dragging her to her feet without a word. Running full out, the dog yowling and scrabbling against the fence behind them.

And she'd never been so scared, so terrified.

She'd never been so certain that she was about to die.

Dotty would be devastated. Bennett would be…

She didn't know how her uncle would feel. It wasn't that they weren't close. It was more that he wasn't invested. Not the way Dotty was. A high-powered defense attorney, he had a large clientele and a very busy life. Even before she'd reached legal maturity, she'd been more of an afterthought to him than a concern.

Radley had her by the wrist and was nearly dragging her as he sprinted across a wide expanse of grass. Odd that out here in the deep woods there were cleared areas and a tall fence. Not something she'd have expected of a serene getaway from civilization.

But then, most of what she'd discovered at the Sanctuary hadn't been what she'd expected. Not that she'd been looking for it to be anything other than the haven Mary Alice had run to.

Radley led her back into a dense forest. She tripped, but he didn't slow his stride. Just tightened his grip on her forearm and kept going. He must have felt what Honor did—danger breathing down their necks, death knocking on their doors.

That definitely sounded like something Dotty would have said when Honor was a young teenager and a college student. Filled with energy and wisdom and funny turns of phrase. Dotty had changed a lot in the past few years. A bout of pneumonia had sent her to the hospital for nearly a month. She'd aged then, returning to the farm but struggling to care for the animals and the property. Since then, Honor had been driving out to the farm after work on Friday and returning to her apartment late Sunday night.

It was exhausting, but Honor hadn't had the heart to suggest that it was time for Dotty to move away from the house she'd lived in for fifty years. Dotty had raised two sons there, nursed her husband through cancer twice, had spent countless hours in the kitchen making meals for her family and for other families in the community.

Thinking about her having to give that up made Honor's chest tight and her eyes burn.

She pushed the thoughts away, focusing on the moment. On the throbbing pain in her hands, the dull ache in her head. Her lungs ached, too, every breath labored as she struggled to keep the wild pace.

She could still hear the dog, his baying muffled by thick trees and the slushing pulse of blood in her ears. Her legs were shaky, her arms weak. If she'd still been carrying the backpack, she'd have been done by now. She glanced at Radley. He was carrying his duffel, wearing the pack and running like he could go all night.

"You're doing great," he said.

"Do you have any idea where we're headed?"

she panted, the breath hot and sharp at the back of her throat.

"Right now? We're just putting some distance between us and them."

"And then what?"

"We move forward with our plan."

"They'll be waiting at the truck. You know that, right?"

"I know that we don't have another option, and with the pistol you got your hands on, I'll have a good chance at getting what I'm going in for."

"*You'll* have a good chance? It seems to me there are two of us here."

"And only one of us has a gun."

"I took it from Absalom, so claiming rights are mine," she pointed out. Not that having the gun would do her any good. Her hands were as close to useless as they could be, and she wouldn't be able to fire the weapon easily.

"You make disarming a man sound easy," he said.

"It was. I shot Absalom full of a sedative he was trying to inject me with. He was out cold in seconds."

"Did you keep the syringe?"

"I was more interested in getting away than in collecting evidence."

"Not for evidence. I'm curious about the

contents. You were out cold when I arrived. I was sitting with you for nearly an hour before you did more than twitch a finger. I thought you were unconscious from the fever. Now I'm wondering if you were drugged."

"I've been wondering the same. I'm just not sure what he had to gain from keeping me here."

"Money? Does Mary Alice have a lot of it?"

"She's a biochemist and works for a pharmaceutical company. She makes great money, and her parents are both doctors. They live in as close to a mansion as a house can get without being one."

"Does she live with them?"

"No. She works in Boston and has a nice house in Saugus. It's not far from where her parents live, and very close to the house where I grew up. The elementary school we attended is right around the corner. That's where we met."

"Mary Alice is your connection to Absalom. I have to believe you being drugged and kept here has something to do with him not wanting you to find her and talk her out of joining his group." He was still moving swiftly, pulling back branches and holding them so that she wouldn't get slapped in the face.

"Mary Alice isn't stupid enough to join a cult."

"Didn't you tell me that she wasn't at The Sanctuary? That she'd left to go to a training facility?"

"Yes, but..."

That was it. Just "but," because she couldn't reconcile the smart, feisty, quick-witted woman she knew with the kind of person she thought would be sucked into a place like Sunrise Spiritual Sanctuary.

He didn't press her, didn't ask her to continue or to explain.

Which was good, because she couldn't. She and Mary Alice had been as close as sisters. Maybe closer. If anyone had asked her a month ago, she'd have said she knew everything there was to know about her friend. All the secrets, all the fears, all the hopes and dreams. But Mary Alice had changed since she'd called off her wedding. She'd become quieter, less willing to share. More difficult to contact. As a matter of fact, prior to Mrs. Stevenson calling to ask if Honor had heard from Mary Alice, it had been weeks since they'd spoken.

She should have called and called and called again until she had finally reached her friend.

She should have asked hard questions.

She should have confronted Mary Alice, asked for an explanation for the distance that was growing between them. Two decades of friendship wasn't something she should have let slide.

"It's not your fault," Radley said.

"What?"

"Whatever you're blaming yourself for. You're not responsible for the choices Mary Alice made, so don't waste energy feeling guilty or wishing you'd done something different."

"This is the third time you've accurately guessed what I was thinking. I feel like you took an extra course during your FBI training. One called *How to Read a Person's Mind.*"

"I'm no mind reader, but I know about guilt. I carried it around for years."

"Guilt over what?"

"It's a long story. One better shared when we're not running for our lives." He stopped, and she realized she could see lights through the trees again. Smaller than the ones on the gate. Higher. Streetlights on tall spindly posts. Jutting up from asphalt.

"I want you to stay here and stay hidden," Radley said.

"I hope you're kidding."

"I don't kid when I'm working," he replied. "I don't think we're going to make it out of here in the truck, but if I can get the phone, I can call Wren for backup."

"Leave the phone. We can find one on our way to town," she argued, because she didn't think walking into the parking lot was the safe or the right choice.

"At one of the houses that are lining the street?" he asked.

She got his point.

Of course she did.

There was nothing out here.

Except danger.

"Radley—"

"Stay hidden. Stay down. I'll be back soon."

He dropped the backpack and duffel near her feet.

"Promise me, Honor. I can't concentrate on what I'm doing if I think you're wandering around putting yourself in danger."

There was something about the way he said it, something about the strength in his gaze as he looked into her eyes that made her nod her head and agree to something she didn't want.

"I promise," she heard herself say.

He walked away before she could take back the words.

Probably because he'd already realized she'd want to.

She crouched behind several bushes, watching his progress as he slipped through the trees and approached the clearing that surrounded the parking area.

She wanted to call him back, but her voice would carry further than his ears, and she couldn't risk drawing the attention of the guard she knew was stationed at the parking lot entrance.

There was a little shack there. Made of rough-hewn wood and a thatched roof. Open on all sides so that the guard's vision wouldn't be obscured.

She'd noticed that when she'd arrived.

It had seemed odd that the owners of the retreat had been so concerned about protecting vehicles parked out in the middle of nowhere. She'd filed that thought away but hadn't allowed it to sway her decision to enter The Sanctuary.

She'd been on a mission to find Mary Alice, and she hadn't been thinking clearly about anything else.

Too focused. Too determined. Too dogmatic.

She'd had more than one boyfriend tell her that. Mostly because she'd so often told her boyfriends that she didn't have time for anything more serious than dinner once a week.

It wasn't that she hadn't appreciated the fact that couples needed to spend time together. It was more that she'd been focused on her goals and her future.

She'd like to believe that the child in her had wanted to make her parents proud and prove that what they'd been pouring into her when they'd died hadn't been wasted.

The reality was, she'd never been interested enough in any of the men she'd dated to want to focus on building a future.

When something sparked her mind, she could focus every bit of herself on it.

And, Sunrise Spiritual Sanctuary and Mary Alice's disappearance into it? That had made her think. It had made her wonder. It had made her determined to find the truth.

Which was probably why Wren had cautioned her, asked her to wait things out and let the authorities deal with making certain Mary Alice was okay. She'd handpicked each member of the FBI Special Crimes Unit. She knew their strengths, and she knew their weaknesses.

She knew that Honor was going to get herself in too deep.

And, of course, she had.

Which meant Radley had to be sent to rescue her.

After they got out of this, she'd be sure to tell them both how sorry she was.

If they got out.

She frowned, inching out from behind the bushes. She wanted a better view of the parking lot. It looked empty, but she had the odd and horrifying feeling that men with guns were hunkered down between the vehicles, waiting for Radley to appear.

She'd promised to stay down and stay hidden.

She hadn't promised to stay put.

She left the backpack and duffel and belly-crawled through dirt and dead leaves. The scent of dark rich earth filled her nose and clung to her skin, the quiet sounds of forest life whispering around her. The night seemed peaceful, content and quiet. No traffic noises. No airplanes zipping overhead. No voices out on the streets or raucous laughter in the dead of night. City life had its perks, but it also had its detriments. After living in the suburbs most of her life, she'd been able to appreciate the boisterous, energetic city vibe.

She thought she could get use to rural living, too. The velvety quiet, the subtle noises, the rustle of leaves and grasses. Nature, exposed and beautiful, waiting to be discovered again.

How many times had Dotty told her to slow down and look around and appreciate God's creation?

Now she had no choice. Lying stomach-down in the dirt, bare feet pressed into cool earth and damp leaves, heart pounding against decayed vegetation, she used her elbows, knees and toes to push through the woods and to the edge of the clearing. She could see better there.

Long grass swayed as a cold breeze swept through, sending leaves skittering across the parking lot. There were no trees nearby. The area had been thoroughly cleared. She could see the guard shack and the metal chain strung between two posts at the entrance of the lot. She'd arrived at midday, but she'd parked beneath a streetlight. She could see her Ford Explorer and the old truck parked beside it. That had to be Radley's vehicle. Funny, she'd have pegged him as more the sports car type.

He'd disappeared, and she tried to find him, scanning the lot and probing the shadows.

She knew he was there, but she couldn't find him. Not slithering across the asphalt on his belly or hunkered down near a vehicle.

Good. If she couldn't see him when she knew he was there, the guard couldn't either.

She counted the seconds, praying silently that he'd make it to his truck, find the phone and return. She needed to believe that things would work out, because if they didn't, there'd be no one to blame but herself.

Something moved near the edge of the lot, the grasses seeming to sway more vigorously. Radley?

It had to be. The grasses stilled, the night went silent.

And, her mind jumped in another direction and to other possibilities.

One of Absalom's men could be there—moving in closer, watching from the shadows, waiting, like a viper, to strike.

She shuddered.

There were a few vehicles close to the area where the grass had swayed. She'd guess there were dozens of eyes watching the lot, several armed men waiting for a shadow to move.

They needed a distraction, something that would draw their attention away from the parking area.

She planned to be it. But, not while dressed in clothes that nearly glowed in the dark.

She crawled back to her pack and dug through it, pulling out black leggings and a dark-colored T-shirt. Her hands hurt enough to steal her breath and make her eyes burn, but she still managed to yank on dark socks and a lightweight pair of black tennis shoes. Her feet hurt, too.

Running barefoot through the woods hadn't been a great idea.

None of this had been.

But she'd made her decisions.

She'd deal with the consequences.

She just wished she hadn't dragged someone else in on it with her.

She frowned, eyeing the area where the grass had moved. Still nothing. She crawled through the foliage, staying close to the tree line, afraid she'd lose her way if she couldn't see the street lights.

When she was perpendicular to where she thought Radley might be, she dropped the bags into thick underbrush, tossing leaves and pine needles over them. Then, she searched the ground for sticks and rocks, collected enough to make some noise, tied them into the hem of her shirt and climbed as far up into a pine tree as she could.

Her palms were bloody, her eyes tearing with pain, but she had a good vantage point, and she was high enough to avoid any bullets that flew her way.

She hadn't stayed down, but she was still hidden. Hopefully, that would be enough to keep them both safe.

The grass was long enough to hide in.

A big mistake if a person were concerned about securing the area. Radley was certain

Absalom was. He didn't know what exactly was being hidden from the world. Maybe just the fact that a spiritual leader and his cult following were living on a posh resort. Maybe something darker.

Radley planned to find out.

Eventually.

Right now, he wanted to get to the truck, retrieve his spare phone and get back to Honor. She'd promised to stay hidden. He hoped she'd follow through. The last thing he wanted was to be caught in the crosshair of a sniper's bullet. And he had a feeling there were snipers stationed at the guard shack and behind the vehicles that were parked close to it.

He'd give them credit for staying still and silent.

But he could feel their presence like the cold wind, like the moisture in the air.

He waited at the edge of the lot, hidden by grass that was weeks past needing to be mowed. Thick and dry from the autumn sun, it swished in the wind, creating its own haunting melody.

There were several cars parked nearby. Fancy BMWs, Cadillacs and sports cars. He could use them as cover. If he could get to them without being seen.

The wind had picked up and clouds skittered across the sky, obliterating starlight and moonglow. The streetlights illuminated the lot, though. He'd need to clear several feet without being spotted.

If he knew how many guards were watching, he could have weighed the risk. Instead, he was working blind. No fellow team members doing reconnaissance or gathering information. No radio contact with a backup team.

He was on his own.

His mother would have chided him for thinking that.

God is always with you, she'd have said.

And she'd have been right.

Of course, she'd also have told him he was an idiot for getting himself into this situation. Ronda Tumberg never pulled her punches. She was the kind of mother everyone should have—funny, smart, quirky and tough. If he acted like a fool, then she told him he was doing it. If he did something idiotic, she didn't hesitate to say so.

In this case, she'd have been right. Again.

The fact was, he could have said no when Wren asked him to make the trip to Vermont. He could have asked her to send one of the other team members, but he'd just closed the file on a sting operation that he'd been working for a year. He'd sent ten people to prison, and he'd been able to look into the eyes of several of their victims, knowing that they finally had a small sense of closure.

But it wasn't enough.

Nothing was ever enough to undo the damage they'd suffered.

He loved his job. He couldn't imagine doing anything else.

But sometimes it got to him.

This last case had been one of those times.

Maybe Wren had known it. Maybe she'd realized how much he'd needed a break from human sickness and filth and sin. He couldn't think of any other reasons she'd have asked him to check on Honor. He certainly wasn't the most diplomatic or empathetic of the team. He'd never spent time with Honor outside of work. Aside from what he'd noticed during meetings and in the office, he knew nothing about her.

As far as he was concerned, he should have been Wren's last resort. But she'd asked him, and he'd said yes. He'd needed a change of pace.

He'd gotten one, but it wasn't anything like what he'd expected. It was too late to back out. He was in things deep, and there was nothing to do but press forward.

He just wasn't sure how to do that without

getting killed or captured. Neither was high on his list of things he wanted to accomplish. Either would mean trouble for Honor.

He needed a distraction. Something to draw the guard's attention away from the parking area. He had the gun in hand, and he could fire a shot, but that would draw them to his hiding place. Whether he liked it or not, making a break for the nearest vehicle was his only option. He eased forward, the rustling grass camouflaged by the cold wind that was blowing through.

He hoped.

He was about to break free of his cover when something crashed through the trees on the western edge of the lot. It skittered and jumped through the leaves and clattered against wood.

He *almost* popped up to take a look.

If he hadn't been so well trained, he probably would have.

Someone shouted. Feet pounded on pavement. Men rushed from behind cars parked near the guard station, racing toward the trees and away from Radley.

And he suddenly knew what had made the sounds.

Who had made them.

Honor.

She hadn't stayed down. She hadn't stayed quiet, and she hadn't kept her promise.

But she'd provided a distraction. He could use it to their advantage, or he could go after the men who were running toward her.

He hesitated for a split second, praying he'd make the right choice. The sounds came again. This time, further away, deeper in the woods.

He stayed low, darted to the closest car and then under it. No bullets flying. No guards running in his direction. Honor had created a clear path between him and the truck.

He moved from vehicle to vehicle as quickly and cautiously as possible. He didn't want to waste the opportunity she'd handed him. Men were shouting, crashing through the wooded area. If he were them, he'd be calling for the bloodhound, requesting backup. The compound's main gate was across a paved road. Not far from the guard shack, and not far enough for Radley's liking.

It wouldn't take long for men to come streaming across the street.

He reached the truck, slid under it. He'd had a small lockbox drilled into the chassis. Invisible unless a person was under the vehicle, it was just large enough to keep a spare key, a spare cell phone, and in this case, his wallet and correct ID.

He unlocked the box, pulled everything out and closed it again. Voices were coming from several directions now, and he thought that guards were arriving from the compound.

He considered climbing into the truck and leading them away, but he couldn't leave Honor behind. Not with a small army of men chasing her through the woods.

He tucked the wallet, key and phone into his interior jacket pocket and slid out from beneath the truck. Even the arriving guards seemed focused on the area the noise had come from. They might be trained paramilitary, but they weren't very good at their jobs.

That wasn't going to work out well for Absalom, but it was working very well for Radley.

He made his way back in the direction he'd come, moving swiftly, the clatter of boots on pavement hiding the sound of his departure. He made it to the grass and headed west. He needed to find Honor before the guards did.

He'd save the lecture he planned to give her until after they were safely away.

FIVE

Obviously, Honor hadn't thought her plan through carefully enough. Climbing a tree and tossing things as far away from her hiding place as she could had seemed like a good idea until right around the time Absalom's men had raced toward her. She could see them, pounding across the grassy field, heading straight in her direction.

She braced herself for discovery, wishing she'd kept one of the rocks as a weapon. Instead, the only thing she had were pine needles and bleeding hands.

A guard crashed through the bushes below her, so close to the backpack and duffel she'd abandoned that she was certain he'd trip over them. He missed by inches, his focus on the forest ahead rather than the canopy of trees above.

She'd gotten that right, at least.

As soon as he disappeared into the woods,

she wanted to jump down and sprint away. Her body itched to move, to put distance between herself and the men who were hunting her.

But she'd promised Radley she'd stay hidden. Running across an open field didn't count as that.

She hoped he'd made it to the truck. She prayed he had. If he got the phone and escaped, they'd both be rescued.

Or, at least, he would.

If she died, it would be her fault for not listening to wise counsel.

There was some irony in that.

Uncle Bennett had often told her she wasn't good at taking advice from people who knew better than her. She'd brushed that off as sour grapes. He'd gotten cranky right around the time she'd become legally responsible for her parents' estate. She'd been twenty-one. Fresh out of college. Probably a little naïve and foolish, but smart and ready for life. Bennett had been trustee of the estate until that point, and she'd figured he hadn't liked giving up control.

Maybe, though, he'd been right.

She did have a habit of making her own decisions regardless of what anyone else thought.

She liked to gather facts and figures, weigh choices and outcomes, make spreadsheets.

She liked to think she had life figured out.

Based on the fact that she was sitting in a tree, a horde of armed men racing past her hiding place, she wasn't sure she was right about that.

One of the men stopped a few feet away, calling something into his radio. Something about dogs and escapees.

Her blood ran cold, her thoughts sharply focused.

She'd forgotten about the bloodhounds.

Her ears strained for signs that the dogs were on the way. It wouldn't take long for them to track her scent. She'd left the pajamas behind, and from there, she'd be easy to trail.

The hounds probably wouldn't even need that.

They'd probably smell her as she sat up in the tree, trot right to her hiding place and bay wildly until their handlers arrived.

The guard moved on, not as quickly as the others. He was looking at the ground, probably trying to find signs that she'd been there. She waited, counting her heartbeats, praying he didn't return. The parking lot looked empty now. Her gaze darted to the area where Radley had been hiding.

Was he still there?

Had he used the distraction to reach the truck?

She couldn't wait around to find out.

She eased down. Slowly. Carefully. As silently as she could. The wind had picked up and cold air seeped through her thin shirt. She shivered, her teeth chattering, her body shaking. She could hear pine needles swishing as she moved. Could anyone else?

Please, God, get me out of this, she prayed.

Her hands were slippery with blood, her feet throbbing.

She tried to ignore both, to focus on the guards, whose voices were growing faint.

She heard the first dog as she reached the ground. Knew that it wouldn't be long before she could see them bounding across the parking lot.

She had no idea which way to go, but she couldn't stay where she was, and she couldn't head deeper into the woods.

She raced into the clearing, leaving the duffel and backpack behind. Hoping they'd entice the dogs.

The parking lot was straight ahead. She veered away from it, aiming in the direction of the road.

She hoped.

She was great at finding her way through computer systems.

She wasn't as good at navigating the real world.

She got lost at least twice a week walking

through her neighborhood. How in the world did she ever imagine she could find her way out of the Vermont wilderness?

In for a penny. In for a pound.

Dotty's voice rang through her head.

She was committed now. She couldn't turn back. Not with the dogs howling in the distance.

Something bounded from the grass to her right, a dark shape that she was sure was a bloodhound.

She didn't scream.

She didn't have time.

One minute she was on her feet, the next she was on the ground, a hard body pressing her into the grass.

"Don't move," a man hissed.

She tried to twist out from beneath him, but he outweighed and outmuscled her.

"I said don't move, Honor," he repeated.

And she finally recognized the voice.

Radley.

"You're okay!" she gasped.

"Don't talk, either," he responded. "Do you understand?"

She nodded, because he'd told her not to speak, and because she was weak with relief, her thoughts fuzzy, her ears buzzing. She closed her eyes, just for a second, listening to voices and howling dogs and the wild beating of her heart.

"Don't pass out on me," Radley whispered, his breath warm against her ear. She opened her eyes, and he was lying beside her, staring into her face.

"Okay," she mumbled.

"The dogs are on leads. Handlers are bringing them to the woods. We can make it out, but we're going to have to be smart. Do you have the pack and duffle?"

"I left everything behind. Including The Sanctuary prison garb."

"That explains why I didn't realize it was you. You changed clothes."

"I thought I'd make it more difficult for them to see me."

"Let's hope it keeps being difficult. Stay here. I'll check things out." He moved away, and she felt the cold, the first drops of rain, the prickly blades of grass poking her skin. She didn't bother levering up to see where he'd gone. She knew he'd return. They were trapped like rats in the middle of an open field, and it was her fault.

She'd have kicked herself if she had the energy to do it.

More rain fell, splattering onto her cheek and bouncing off the ground nearby. It muffled the sound of Absalom's men and their dogs. She nearly raised her head, then, to look around and see if there might be an easy route out of the field, but Radley had warned her to stay down. This time, she was determined to listen.

She didn't hear him return. She felt him, sliding through the grass nearby. When he touched her shoulder, she wasn't surprised.

"The good news is, we've got a chance," he whispered. "Looks like they've all headed into the woods and left the parking lot unattended. I already have the key to the truck. All we have to do is get to it, and we can ride out of here in style. The bad news is, the dogs are going to find the things you left behind and track you out of the woods. Once we poke our heads up, we're going to have to book it to the vehicle."

"That doesn't sound like bad news to me," she whispered back, and he grinned, his eyes crinkling in the corners.

"That's what I was hoping you'd say. Ready?"

He had her wrist and was pulling her upright before she could form a thought. Then they were sprinting full-out, racing across the open field as rain poured from the sky and a bloodhound bayed.

* * *

Honor ran beside him, gasping for breath but keeping pace. Radley hoped that meant she hadn't been injured when he'd tackled her. He'd realized who she was seconds before they'd hit the ground, and he'd tried to pull back, roll sideways to take some of the force from the fall, but he knew he'd knocked the air from her lungs. He should have recognized her. He probably would have, but he'd been staying low, listening more than watching the activity. He'd heard her moving. She hadn't been quiet about it, sprinting across the field as if she knew exactly where she was headed.

He'd levered up just enough to see a dark shape against the steely sky. He hadn't waited to see more. He'd pounced, realizing his mistake a few seconds too late.

She'd been smart to change clothes. Smart to leave things in the woods. She'd even been smart to make a run for the road. There was no way she'd have escaped on foot, though. Not with the bloodhounds on the ground and her scent everywhere. They'd have hunted her down before she'd made it a third of the distance to town.

No, the best option was going for the truck.

That had its risks, too, but maybe not as many.

They reached the edge of the lot, and he

could see the truck, her Explorer beside it, the streetlight glowing softly on the hoods of the vehicles.

Behind them, the bloodhounds sounded the alarm. Time was running out. Quickly.

"We're almost there," he said, picking up the pace, because he could. She tripped but kept going, panting and wheezing, gasping for air.

He scooped her up, tossing her over his shoulder like one of the sacks of chicken feed he used to have to haul to the henhouse after his parents had moved the family from the city to the rural property they'd been dreaming of for years.

Honor didn't protest.

That worried him almost as much as the voices that were shouting behind them. Cries to halt, to stop, to freeze. The men were armed, and he expected them to take a shot as soon as they were close enough.

"They're coming!" Honor warned. "Put me down and get the truck!"

"We're here." He snagged the key from his pocket, unlocked the door and nearly tossed her inside. She scrambled over the middle console, and he had the engine running before she was in her seat.

"Get down!" he shouted, as he gunned the engine and took off.

She did, curling her upper body around her legs, still panting, gasping and wheezing.

The muffled sound of a gunshot drifted into the cab, but they'd already cleared the empty guard shack, were flying past the compound gate. Men were running through the parking lot, guns drawn, firing at air because the truck was already out of range. He didn't let up on the accelerator. Absalom's men had vehicles, and they could follow easily.

He sped around a curve in the road, heading south toward town. There were no lights on this stretch of highway, no houses, no signs of civilization. He pulled out his cell phone, speed-dialing Wren's number.

She answered immediately. "Santino here. Did you find her?"

"I found her and a lot of trouble."

"For some reason that doesn't surprise me. Is she hurt?"

"I'm fine," Honor mumbled, obviously able to hear both sides of the conversation.

"She's injured. I'm going to take her to the nearest hospital, but I need backup, and I need you to send the state police to close down Sunrise Spiritual Sanctuary and arrest Absalom Winslow. He runs the place."

"Charges?"

"Kidnapping with intent to do bodily harm.

False imprisonment. Give me some time, and I might be able to dig up some more charges."

"That'll be enough. What else do you need?"

"The name of the local hospital and a clear route to get there."

"You're on your backup phone?"

"Yes."

"I'm pulling up GPS coordinates. Give me five minutes, and I'll call you back with the information you need."

"Thanks, Wren." He disconnected, glancing in his rearview mirror. Still no sign of a tail.

"I don't need to go to a hospital." Honor's head popped up, and she swiveled in her seat, looking through the back window.

"Anyone looking at you would argue that you did."

"I can't look that bad." She flipped down the visor and looked in the vanity mirror. "Okay. Maybe I do."

That surprised a laugh out of him. "You're an interesting person, Honor."

"Thanks. I think."

"It is a compliment. Maybe that's why Absalom wanted to keep you around. He was taking a huge risk when he decided not to let a federal officer leave. He had to have known you'd be missed."

"I fudged my personal information when I

filled out the retreat application. I said I lived at my grandmother's place and helped her with the farm."

"I'm surprised that got you entrance. I thought they wanted wealthy clientele."

"They want any clientele that can pay their exorbitant fees. Plus, my grandmother's farm is worth a pretty penny. It's in a prime location. Forty miles outside of Boston. I also inherited money from my parents when they died. I made sure to mention that. Put in a little blurb about trying to figure out where I fit in the world now that they're gone."

"I didn't realize both your parents had died. I'm sorry for your loss," he said, surprised that he hadn't heard about it through the grapevine at work. The team was family. One person's suffering was the group's.

"It was a long time ago, Radley. I was twelve."

"That's a hard age to lose your parents."

"Any age is a hard age for that."

She had a point. He lived hundreds of miles away from his folks, but they filled a spot in his life, his heart and his thoughts that no one else could.

"Did Dotty raise you after they passed away?"

"Yes. And no. My father's brother was my legal guardian. Bennett is a criminal defense attorney in Boston. He was in high demand. Even when I was a kid, so Dotty stepped in and did most of the parenting."

"Bennett Remington is your uncle?" He knew the name, had seen the smarmy commercials, faced the guy in court a couple of times.

"Yes. You know him?"

"We've been across the courtroom from each other a few times."

"I'm sure you were impressed by his astounding knowledge of the law and his lack of discernment when it comes to choosing his clients," she said, and there was no mistaking the disdain in her voice.

"I take it the two of you don't get along?"

"We get along."

"But?"

"We don't see eye to eye on a few issues. Namely, the fact that he earns a lot of money getting guilty men off on technicalities and that he's made his fortune protecting white collar criminals who deserve to be in jail for what they've done."

"He might argue that everyone has the right to legal defense."

"He might, but he and I don't argue. He's not concerned with my opinion of his work, and I'm not concerned about his opinion of mine." Honor was still twisted in her seat, looking out the back window. The instrument panel lights shone on her cheek, her arm and hand. There was blood on her fingers. Not a little of it, either.

"Your hand is bleeding. There's a first aid kit in the glove compartment," he said. "What's with your uncle? He doesn't value your job?"

She shrugged. "My father was a police officer. My mother was a lawyer. I don't think my uncle has any thought one way or another about what I do. We're related. He'd help me if I needed it. That's about as far as it goes." She paused, shifted a little further in her seat. "There's a car coming. I can see its lights."

He glanced in his review mirror, saw the headlights.

"They don't give up easily," he muttered.

"Apparently not," she replied, grabbing her seat belt and snapping it on.

"I'd like to know what they're after. Aside from you."

"How about we figure that out after we've left them in our dust?" she suggested.

He nodded, accelerating into the next curve, all his focus on the road, on maintaining control of the truck, on getting as far away from the approaching vehicle as fast as he could.

Because backup still hadn't arrived, and until it did, he and Honor were outarmed and outnumbered.

SIX

Slow down!

Be careful!

We're going to die!

She wanted to shout a dozen warnings, beg Radley to slow down, explain that she'd just as soon not die in a fiery explosion of twisted metal.

They were moving at breakneck speed, taking curves so fast that she was certain the tires on her side of the truck lifted from the pavement.

She kept her mouth shut, though.

She was afraid to break Radley's concentration.

She was also afraid that if they slowed down, they'd be caught, recaptured and killed.

Why? What was it Absalom hoped to accomplish?

Those were questions she and Radley both wanted answers to.

They reached the end of the road, blew through a stop sign and out onto the state highway. There were lights here but still no vehicles.

Radley pulled into the left lane, gave the wheel a sharp turn and bounced over the grassy median. They were heading the opposite direction, speeding toward the road they'd just exited. She saw lights as they passed, but the driver would have no idea she and Radley had done a U-turn.

Radley passed another exit and another, trees whipping by, rain splattering on the windshield. The storm had arrived. Not just a few drops of rain. A downpour splattering onto the asphalt and bouncing in the truck's headlights.

If a deer or moose darted out in front of them, if a slow-moving vehicle took an on-ramp and cut them off, if any number of things happened, Radley would have to slam on his brakes, the truck would spin out and they'd crash.

"I think it's safe to slow down," she said, her voice a high-pitched squeak that would have embarrassed her if she hadn't been so frightened.

"You're scared," he commented, but he

eased off the gas, slowed down to a more reasonable speed.

"Terrified is a better adjective."

"Remember the defensive driving course every FBI agent has to take?"

"Yes."

"I passed it."

"That's comforting, Radley."

He chuckled. "I just thought you should know. In case we've got to speed out of a dangerous situation again."

"My father passed a defensive driving class, too. He and my mother were killed in a single-car accident three miles from home. It was raining. The roads were wet. The police think my dad swerved to avoid an animal. He lost control. The car spun out, and he hit a tree. He died instantly. My mother died at the hospital a few hours later." The words poured out because she really was terrified, and she couldn't seem to stop them.

"I'm sorry, Honor. I had no idea."

"How would you? Up until tonight, I don't think we've ever exchanged more than a few words."

"I've been thinking about that, and wondering why not," he said, slowing the truck even more. There was something comforting about Radley. Something steady and confident and certain. Solid. Dependable. Those were words people at work had used to describe him. Seeing him in a crisis, watching his calm determination, she could understand why.

"Why not what?" she asked, her throat tight with longing that she recognized for what it was: a desire to be part of a couple, to have someone standing in her corner who wanted to be there no matter what. Her parents had had that. Her grandparents. But Honor had always been too busy for relationships. She'd always felt smothered by the expectations that seemed inherent in romantic entanglements. Now, though, she felt hollow with loneliness and more aware than she wanted to be of just how few connections she had. She wanted the kind of bond that mattered, the deep and abiding love that would last a lifetime. She hadn't realized how much.

Not when she went out to dinner with one guy after another, searching for something that she never quite found. Not when she was home late at night, staring at the ceiling fan as it whirled above her, wondering why she suddenly felt so alone.

She liked her life just the way it was.

She'd been telling herself that for years.

She was busy, successful, fulfilled.

She had no room for anything else.

But, she could *make* room for what her parents had had. She could bundle up the rest of her world and shove it aside, just a little, to make space for that kind of relationship.

"Why do we not chat at work?" Radley said. "We talk to other people there."

"We work different angles, Radley," she reminded him. "I'm in the office. You're in the field."

"I'm not always in the field. And, we're both on the same team, pursuing the same goal. That gives us a lot in common."

"I suppose it does," she replied, opening his glove compartment and looking for the first aid kit he'd mentioned, because her hand *was* bleeding, and because thinking about that was easier than thinking about the reasons why her cheeks were suddenly hot.

"We also both work out at the office gym," he continued.

"True." She found the kit and set it on her lap, but her fingers were swollen and stiff from burns and healing infection. She couldn't manage the catch that held it closed.

"And, I've seen the package of cookies you keep on your desk. We obviously both like to eat."

"I do like food," she agreed, knowing he was trying to distract her from the rain, the road and her own fear, and liking him more because of it.

More than she had before he'd come to find her.

More than she had five minutes ago.

More, even, than maybe she should.

"Do you need help with that?" he asked.

"What?"

"The first aid kit. Want me to open it for you?"

"I'd rather you keep both hands on the wheel."

"Should I mention the defensive driving course again?"

"Should I mention the fact that this truck is a lot more powerful than it looks, and I'd rather not die?"

He laughed, reaching over and flicking the kit open.

"Worry steals today of its pleasures," he commented.

"First," she retorted, taking alcohol wipes from the kit and using them to wipe the blood from her hands. "There is nothing pleasurable about today. Second, I'm not worried. I'm just pointing out the fact that I'd rather not die. Third, I didn't take you for the philosophical type."

"What type did you take me for?"

"I hadn't really given it much thought. But, probably driven. Determined. Black-and-white."

"Yes. To all those. My mother is more the philosophical type. The worry thing is one of her favorite sayings."

"She sounds like an interesting lady."

"She is. How are your hands?" He exited the freeway, bouncing along a rutted ramp and onto a country road. No change in his facial expression, but he glanced in the review and side mirrors, his muscles just a little tenser than they'd been seconds ago.

"They hurt." She shifted in her seat, looking out the back of the vehicle.

The road was empty, the pavement dark.

He accelerated, his speed just a little too fast for the darkness of the road and the weather conditions.

"Are we being followed?" she asked.

"I don't think so."

"Think?"

"I've seen no sign of a tail, but getting off the main road will give me a clearer view. If I find a place to pull over, I'll call Wren. I want to make certain there's nothing going on that we should know about."

"I am fairly certain there is a lot going on that we should know about," she said, still staring out the back window, her hands throbbing in time with her heartbeat, her mind sifting and sorting pieces of information.

Mary Alice had entered The Sanctuary willingly.

She'd stayed willingly.

She'd gone to training to become a member of Absalom's group.

Willingly?

Probably.

She'd never been one to do anything she didn't want to. She'd never been prone to emotionalism, loneliness or depression.

"I meant that if there's anything going on with the local authorities," he corrected. "It would give me a lot of pleasure to know that the police have closed down The Sanctuary. As for anything else, there's a boatload of stuff going on in The Sanctuary that we need to know about."

"The resort part of the operation is on the up-and-up," she said. "Very nice accommodations, great food, lots of interesting classes designed to slow people down and get them more in tune with nature."

"And, convince them to give up their wealth and join Absalom's group?"

"Probably. I wasn't handed a lot of propaganda. But, then, I wasn't pretending to be ultra-wealthy, either."

"You researched before you came to Vermont." It wasn't a question, but she answered anyway.

"Yes. And I didn't find much about Absalom or his group. It's a cult of some sort, but there's no internet presence, no complaints to the Better Business Bureau, no former members doing tell-alls with the press."

"How about Sunrise Spiritual Sanctuary? As far as the resort goes, any complaints?"

"None."

"So people are happy with their experience there."

"What's not to be happy about? As I said, everything they promise, they deliver on."

"Except that some people end up with burned hands and memory loss," he pointed out.

"I was asking a lot of questions."

"About?"

"Mary Alice. The group. The people who are actually members of it."

"And, you think you got under Absalom's skin, and that he decided to keep you from doing any more digging?"

"I don't know. I can't remember how this happened." She lifted her hands, let them fall back into her lap.

"That's strange, don't you think?"

"Yes."

"So, we need to figure out what happened to your hands. We need to find out why your questions might have been making Absalom uncomfortable."

"We need to find Mary Alice. That's my priority. It was when I arrived. It still is."

"You said she's at a training facility?"

"In Boston. Or the vicinity of it. I planned to leave here and head back home. But that never happened."

"We'll be back there soon." He turned into what had once been a paved lot. Now, it was cracked bits of asphalt mostly hidden by grass and debris.

Up ahead, a building sat on the tangled lot, its roof caved in and partially missing, its ragged siding slick with rain. The windows had been boarded up, but most of the boards were hanging loose, revealing triangles of the interior darkness.

"This is just about the creepiest place I've ever seen," she whispered without meaning to.

"Abandoned schools usually are."

"How do you know it was a school?"

"The sign." He pointed to a crumbling brick structure that stood near the edge of the lot. A sign had been attached to it years ago, the letters so faded she could only make out S-C-H-O-O-L.

"A school for who? There's nothing out here."

"That's probably why the school is in this condition." He parked the truck beneath the low-hanging boughs of a maple tree, turning off the engine and flipping on the interior light. "Go ahead and bandage your hands. I'll check out the area, and then call Wren."

"Check out what part of the area? There's nothing here," she said, but he'd already opened the door and was stepping out into the rain and wind.

Obviously, he had something to say to Wren that he didn't want her to hear.

Just as obviously, she wasn't going to sit in the vehicle bandaging her hands while he did it.

Whatever he had to say, she planned to hear it.

She opened the door and walked around the vehicle, following him as he made his way to the old school house.

Radley dialed Wren's number as he reached the crumbling façade of the building.

As schools went, this one hadn't been much of one. Two-story. Rectangular. At its peak, it may have housed a few hundred children. Now, it was probably home to more than that many rats, squirrels, bats and birds.

He stayed outside, standing under a broken covered entryway, chilly rain dripping down his head and onto his cheeks.

Honor had followed him and was standing so close their shoulders brushed as she turned to survey their surroundings.

He didn't tell her to go back to the truck.

He knew she wouldn't.

Just like he knew that Wren wasn't going to pick up when she hadn't after the first three rings. He let it go to voicemail, left a brief message with the coordinates of their location, and shoved his phone into his pocket.

"No answer?" Honor asked, her teeth chattering. Her entire body was shaking.

He frowned, dragging her an inch closer, so they were side by side, pressed together, sharing warmth. "You should have stayed in the truck," he commented.

"So that you could discuss the case without me hearing? That wasn't going to happen."

"So that you didn't freeze," he responded, keeping his voice light, his grip lighter as he urged her back to the vehicle.

"What gives you the idea that I'm cold?"

she said, her voice vibrating with the force of her shivers.

"The teeth-chattering thing is a dead giveaway," he responded.

"I was joking, Radley."

"So was I."

"So, you do have a sense of humor," she said with a quiet chuckle that hinted at the amusement and enthusiasm he'd noticed in her eyes when they'd crossed paths at the office.

He liked that about her. The way that nothing ever seemed to get her down. No matter how tough a case was, Honor was always gung-ho about finding answers.

"This surprises you because...?" he asked, and she smiled.

"You're always so serious at the office."

"Not always." They'd reached the truck, and he climbed into the bed, opening the combination lock on the storage box that he'd attached there.

"Every time I see you, you are."

"I think we've established that we don't see each other enough," he replied, not really thinking about what he was saying or how it sounded until the words were out, and she'd gone silent.

"Don't worry, that wasn't an invitation to spend more time together when this is over," he continued, pulling out blankets and a large first aid kit. The other one contained essentials. This one had large gauze bandages that Honor could use to cover her burns.

"I didn't think it was."

"No? You sure went silent fast," he replied, jumping down and grabbing her wrist, hurrying her back to the passenger side of the truck and helping her into her seat.

He hadn't meant the comment as an invitation.

Not even close.

He'd been down that path before. He'd been so close to getting married that he'd spent money on a wedding ring, a venue and a tux. He'd been haggling with his fiancée, Mackenzie, over things like guests and budget. He'd thought he was heading into forever.

Until he'd returned from an overseas military tour and she'd announced that he'd have to give up his military career if they were going to be happy together. She couldn't handle his work schedule. She didn't like being alone. She wanted long lazy weekends with him. Not snippets of life shared when he wasn't gone.

It had been an ultimatum.

He'd been twenty-three. Young enough that he'd almost believed that if he caved into her desires, they could be happy together.

Almost.

In the end, he'd realized that true love didn't demand that a person give up who and what he was for the sake of the relationship.

He'd refused to give up his military career.

Mackenzie had given him back the engagement ring.

A few months later, he'd heard that she was engaged again.

He'd been happy for her. He'd been just as happy for himself. Relationships were hard work. They required commitment, sacrifice and time.

Those were things he gave to his job, because it demanded them. In relationships, Radley preferred to be light, easy and uncomplicated. Dinner once a week. Maybe a movie. No late-night phone calls or early morning coffee dates. He liked his life the way it was.

But, for a moment, looking into Honor's eyes, seeing that hint of amusement and enthusiasm, he couldn't help wondering if there was room for something more.

"It's a little difficult to talk with my teeth chattering so much," she responded to his comment, and the strange spell that seemed to hold him there—standing in the rain, looking into her eyes—was broken.

He nodded, stepped back, closed the door.

Hurried around the vehicle, rain soaking through his clothes, dripping down his face as he climbed into the truck and cranked up the heat.

"Want to share?" she asked, holding out an edge of the blanket.

He had another one, tucked under his arm with the first aid kit.

Probably as soaked as he was.

"I have a jacket behind the seat," he responded, setting the first aid kit and soaked blanket on the center console and grabbing the jacket.

He could have shared that blanket with her.

If they'd been stuck there for the night, maybe he would have.

But, he had the strange feeling that would be a mistake.

That sharing one thing might lead to sharing more.

That getting to know Honor better might lead to wanting to know more.

That was a dangerous path for a die-hard bachelor to travel. He had no intention of walking down it.

"There are gauze wraps in here. Want some help getting bandages on your hands?" he asked, opening the kit and focusing on something other than the woman in the seat beside him.

"I think I'll just let them air out." She flipped her hands so they were palm up and stared at the red and swollen flesh.

She'd been burned badly.

He could see that.

He wanted to know how.

And why.

Because he didn't think it had been an accident.

"Looks like you have second-and third-degree burns."

"Feels like I have one-hundred-degree burns." She smiled, but her face was pale, the freckles on her nose and cheeks standing out in stark contrast. "Interesting thing… Absalom said I fell into a clay-firing pit."

"What's that?"

"Pretty much what it sounds like. Community members throw pots and then fire them the old-fashioned way. Digging pits into the ground, covering them with dirt and placing burning coals on top of it. It's a fascinating process."

"Unless you land in the pit?"

"Right. Absalom said I tripped and landed in one. But that doesn't make a lot of sense to me. I may not be the most athletic person God ever created, but I'm not prone to falling into pits filled with burning coals."

"I'd imagine anyone would be cautious around them," he commented, trying to think of a situation that would have landed Honor on hot coals.

He couldn't, and that made him certain that it hadn't been an accident.

"And, if it was an accident and the burns were this bad," she said and lifted her hands, "why not call for an ambulance, have me transported to a hospital? Why risk a lawsuit?"

"Because, he never intended for you to make it out of the compound?" he suggested, and she frowned.

"That's where the rabbit hole seems to be leading, but Absalom has no reason to kill me. Sure, I was asking questions about the facility and about Mary Alice, but it's not like I found out information that could close down Sunrise Spiritual Sanctuary."

"Does he know you're with the FBI?"

"Not unless he did some deep digging. As you know, that's not information I post on social media. It's certainly not something anyone other than my closest friends and family would know."

"Mary Alice knew," he pointed out.

"Why would she mention it?"

"That's a good question. I have dozens more, but we're not going to get answers sitting here. We need to get you to a hospital."

"I think we should head back to Boston. Get to the field office and regroup there."

"Thanks for sharing your thoughts," he commented, using his phone to find the nearest hospital and pulling up the directions to it.

"But you're going to ignore them?" she asked as he reached over and grabbed the ends of her seatbelt, snapping them into place.

"Ignoring would mean a lack of acknowledgement. I'm acknowledging your thoughts, and I'm going with my own. The sooner your hands are treated, the sooner you can be back at work, and we need you there. The office hasn't been the same without you in it."

That was true.

All of it.

He'd grown accustomed to walking into the office, hearing Honor humming quietly while she worked, her fingers tapping the keyboard as he raced from one case to another.

He hadn't realized how much that had become part of his routine until she'd disappeared for two weeks.

"We can accomplish things a lot more quickly if we get to Boston as soon as possible. Plus, there's a hospital there."

"And Wren is probably already on her way to us. We'll end up passing her on the trip, and it'll take a few more hours to connect. She's expecting us to go to the nearest hospital. That's what I'm planning to do."

"People die at hospitals," she said almost absently as he pulled onto the road.

"People die in lots of places," he pointed out.

"You have a bad habit of being right, Radley. I'm not sure how I feel about that."

"Why is being right a bad habit?"

"It makes other people wrong," she replied, and he laughed.

Something he didn't do as often as he probably should. The endless cases of evil and human avarice made him look at life seriously, view it through a lens of suspicion.

Mackenzie had told him that when he was still in the military working as an MP—*You're no fun anymore. You're too serious.*

Maybe.

But life was serious business. At least, that's what he'd told her.

There had to be a place for fun in it, though.

There had to be a time when laughter welled up and joy reigned and all the terrible things he'd seen and heard were overshadowed by happiness.

"I don't recall saying you were wrong," he

said, and she smiled, her eyes crinkling at the corners, her lips twitching in what might have been the beginning of laughter.

"As I said, the mere act of you being right makes me wrong. But I'll forgive you. If you lend me your phone so that I can call my grandmother."

"You know it's one in the morning, right?" he said, fishing the phone out of his pocket and dropping it in her lap.

"Dotty won't mind," she replied, fumbling to dial with her swollen burned fingers.

He lifted the phone again. "What's the number?"

He dialed as she dictated, then turned the phone on speaker and dropped it in her lap again.

The phone rang twice, and a woman's voice filled the truck.

"Hello?" she nearly shouted.

"Dotty?" Honor responded. "It's me."

"Who is 'me'?"

"Honor. Your granddaughter?" Honor said.

"Honey! I don't need to be reminded of our relationship. I didn't recognize the phone number, and the fact that you called me Dotty… Shame on you for that and for not contacting me in weeks! I've been waiting for you to call. Where have you been?"

"I was looking for—"

"Mary Alice. I know that, but you were supposed to check in every few days. I haven't heard from you once. Bennett said you'd called him and told him things were fine, but I just couldn't believe that you'd call your uncle and not check in with me."

"I…didn't have a phone. Things were a little crazy, and I lost track of time. But I'm fine. I just wanted to let you know that. Everything is okay, and I'll be home soon."

"Very soon, I hope. The people you hired to help me out are great, but I miss you, dear. I miss our walks and watching you ride Bandit. And Wilbur. He's put up such a fuss since you've been gone. Keeps going over to the neighbors to complain about the situation. Then, yesterday, one of the deacons came for a visit, and Wilbur went after him."

"Wilbur has never liked strangers, Grandmom. You know that. You need to sit him down and explain that deacons aren't strangers. They're friends."

"Stop trying to be funny, Honor. Wilbur and I both miss you terribly, and we need you home."

"I know, and I'll be there as soon as I can. I'll call you every day until I get back. I promise."

"You promised before and look what happened. I've aged twenty years worrying about you."

"That would put you at over a hu—"

"Don't even say it. Don't you dare! I'm still claiming forty-nine years on all my health forms."

Honor chuckled, the sound as warm as a fire on a cold winter day. "Do you think they believe it? Considering that you actually have to provide your birthdate?"

"Who cares what they believe? It's me who has to have faith in my youthfulness. After all, I need to live long enough to see you married, and at the rate you're going—"

"How about we discuss my marital status when I get home, okay?"

"If you get home," Dotty responded darkly.

"I'll make sure she does, Ms. Dotty," Radley said, cutting into their conversation as he merged back onto the state highway. The nearest hospital was in Hartford. That should be thirty miles straight up the road.

"Who's that?" Dotty shouted. "You didn't tell me you were traveling with a gentleman friend, Honor."

"I'm Radley Tumberg. A coworker of hers."

"Did Wren send you? I did ask her to check on Honor."

"She did."

"Wonderful. So you're bringing Honor home?"

"Soon," he said.

"Nothing is soon enough when you're my age. I could be dead before soon arrives."

"Gran, you just said you were forty-nine," Honor reminded her, the laughter in her voice obvious.

"I said I was putting that on my medical forms. But when you're lying in bed, listening to the empty house and realizing how alone you are, you start to feel ancient. I'm sure you know that, Radley. Don't you? I'm sure that if you had a grandmother—"

"I do."

"I'm sure you wouldn't let her house be sold out from under her or force her into a retirement home."

"I'd never do that," Honor protested, all the amusement gone from her voice.

"That's not what Bennett said."

"What did he say?"

"Only that you have discussed me moving out of this house."

"And into my apartment. We'd still be at the

farm every weekend. You and I have discussed it. Remember?"

"Of course, I remember. But whatever the plan, it won't be the same as being in the house where I was a young bride and a mother." Dotty sniffed, but Radley had a feeling her eyes were dry.

"I'll get her home to you as soon as I can manage it, Ms. Dotty. Hopefully, we'll get a chance to meet then," he said.

"Yes. Well, it all depends on if I'm here or in some old people's home. I wouldn't want you to see me there. Sitting in a wheelchair, not in control of my faculties."

"Grandmom, stop exaggerating," Honor said tiredly.

Dotty must have heard the exhaustion in her voice. "Are you okay, sweetheart? You don't sound like yourself."

"I'm fine. Just tired, and I still haven't spoken to Mary Alice. Have her parents contacted you?"

"Every day. Her mother is frantic, and I haven't been able to tell them anything except that I'll pray."

"When they call again, tell them that I'm heading back to Boston. Mary Alice is at a training seminar near there. I'll contact them as soon as I get to town."

"All right, dear. You get some sleep, okay? I love you."

"I love you, too, Grandmom." She disconnected and set the phone on the center console.

"She's quite a character," Radley said.

"She is that."

"Is Wilbur your grandfather?"

She laughed quietly, leaning her head back against the seat, her hands palm up on her thighs. "He's her pig. She adopted him from the local kill shelter. He'd been there for a couple of weeks, and she went in with a friend who was looking for a kitten. There he was. A tiny little thing, squealing loudly enough to wake the dead. They told her he was potbellied pig, would never be bigger than a small cat and could live in house. She didn't want him euthanized, so she brought him home. He started growing and just kept on doing it. Now he weighs about two hundred pounds. When he feels ornery, he escapes his pen and goes to the neighbor's property to dig through their trash."

"He sounds like a character, too."

He passed an entrance ramp and frowned as blue-and-white emergency lights cut on. A police car pulled in behind him, following closely enough that he knew it wasn't trying to pass.

He hadn't been speeding. He hadn't broken any laws.

The fact that he was being pulled over anyway made him wary, but one of Wren's cardinal rules was that they follow procedure and cooperate with all local authorities. He had his wallet. He had his ID. He had a gun.

He had an obligation to pull over.

He put on his blinker, pulled into the breakdown lane and coasted to a stop.

"He's not really stopping us, is he?" Honor asked, her gaze focused on the side mirror.

The cruiser pulled in behind them. State police from the looks of it.

"It looks like he is."

"For what?"

"I don't know."

"I don't like this, Radley."

"Neither do I," he replied, but he rolled down his window, pulled out his ID and waited for the officer to get out of his car.

SEVEN

Even before her parents' deaths, hospitals had never been Honor's thing. She'd visited her grandfather when he was ill and remembered sitting in a vinyl-covered chair watching television as her parents talked quietly. She'd been young. Maybe six or seven. Even then, she'd realized that hospitals weren't a place anyone would want to be. The day of the accident, she'd been pulled out of second period and brought to the principal's office. Her uncle had been waiting there, grim-faced and stiff, dressed in the suit and tie he always wore to court. He'd told her about the accident, explained that her father was dead and that her mother was in the hospital.

Just like that.

No couching it with kind words or gentle phrases. No easing into it.

Afterwards, when she'd been old enough to understand better, she'd realized that he'd been in shock. That he'd suddenly been entrusted with a responsibility no one should ever have. That he'd probably had no idea how to approach a child with such devastating news.

At the time, though, she hadn't believed him. Not until he'd driven her to the hospital and walked her into the ICU room where her mother lay. Dotty was standing near the bed, tears streaming down her face. She'd lost her son. She'd probably known she would lose her daughter-in-law, too.

Honor had looked at her mother's swollen and bruised face, and she'd finally understood that everything her uncle had told her was true.

All these years later, she could still remember the way the room had smelled, she could still hear the quiet beep of machines, the soft hiss of the air being pumped into her mother's lungs. She could still feel the shock and the grief.

And she still hated hospitals.

She sat on the edge of the hospital bed, bare feet dangling above the glossy floor. If she'd had her way, she'd have had the officer who'd pulled them over escort them to the state line rather than to the nearest hospital.

Unfortunately, she hadn't had her way. She hadn't had any say, either. Officer Damien Wallace had been contacted by Wren, asked to locate Radley's vehicle and escort it to the nearest hospital.

He'd complied and had seemed eager to hear what they had to say about Absalom Winslow and The Sanctuary. Apparently, this was the first complaint he'd received about the group, but he was suspicious of The Sanctuary's secrecy, curious about what was being hidden there and hoping to make this the last complaint he had about the group.

He liked order and peace.

He liked knowing that people were safe in the area where he worked.

He didn't like having groups like Absalom's making a home in Vermont.

At least, that's what he'd said before he'd gotten in his cruiser and led them to the hospital.

That had been three hours ago. Since then, she'd been pumped full of painkillers, had her wounds cleaned and debrided, been admitted to the hospital and hooked to an IV that was pumping high-powered antibiotics into her system. She'd had blood taken and answered dozens of questions asked by at least three different police officers. She'd talked to her uncle, updated him on the situation, asked if he'd give her legal counsel if she needed it.

Not that she'd thought she would, but she

had stabbed Absalom with a hypodermic needle. If he'd died from the sedation, she might have to prove self-defense.

Bennett had asked a few questions, told her that he'd contact the state police and instructed her to stay safe.

Typical Bennett.

She'd hung up, allowed the nurse to take her temperature for what seemed like the hundredth time, and then it had all been over. The noise. The chaos. People moving in and out of the room.

She'd been left alone, her hands bandaged and nearly pain-free, a thick blanket tossed over her legs. Pillows behind her head, a muted television screen flickering silent sitcoms.

She could have drifted off if she'd let herself, but she was waiting for Radley to walk into the room. He couldn't be far. He'd been there when the attending physician had arrived to do the debriding. He'd asked Honor if she'd wanted him to stay, and when she'd said she didn't, he'd told her he'd be right outside. She couldn't imagine him taking off without letting her know. Unless the police had forced him to go to the station and give his statement there.

Or maybe they'd asked him to return to the Sanctuary and identify the men who'd chased them through the woods.

The thought was more alarming than she wanted it to be.

The entire time she'd been dealing with doctors, nurses and the police, she'd imagined him outside in the hall. She'd thought they weren't farther than a stone's throw from one another. She'd figured that if there was trouble, they'd have each other's back.

Who was she kidding?

She'd been counting on *him* having *her* back.

She'd felt weak as a kitten when she'd arrived, foggy-headed and burning with fever. She'd barely known up from down and had flubbed her statement so badly that Officer Wallace had kindly asked if she'd prefer to give it after she'd been treated.

She'd agreed, because she'd wanted to get things right.

She'd wanted to be sure all the details were there.

She'd wanted Absalom behind bars before he hurt anyone else.

She scooted off the bed, dragging the IV pole across the room. She'd been asked to change into a hospital gown, but she'd refused, kicking off her shoes and socks, and telling anyone who cared to listen that she was happy to stay in her damp clothes.

In retrospect, it probably hadn't been a reasonable choice, but she hadn't cared about being reasonable. She'd cared about getting the treatment over with and leaving.

She hated hospitals almost as much as she hated injustice, but she *did* hate injustice more. If Absalom wasn't arrested and charged with something, no justice would be served.

She frowned, grabbing her shoes and socks from a chair where a nurse had placed them and slipping them on. She felt tired, but better. Less feverish and not shivering with cold. The fact that her hands didn't hurt helped, but she thought the IV drip was doing its job, the antibiotic killing off the bacteria that had invaded her blood.

Twenty-four hours. Maybe forty-eight.

That was how long the doctor had said she needed to stay.

She planned on leaving as soon as she could get the IV out. First, though, she wanted to find Radley. She crossed the room, opened the door, stepped into the hall and straight into his broad chest.

She knew it was him. Without looking at his face. Without him speaking a word. She knew the feel of his hands on her waist, the whisper of his breath in her hair.

"What are you doing out here?" he asked, his fingers warm through her shirt.

"Looking for you."

"You're supposed to be sleeping."

"I can't sleep until I know Absalom is behind bars."

"That might take longer than either of us hoped."

"Why?"

"The state police have been to the compound. They had a search warrant and entered the premises. There was no sign of Absalom. They did arrest several men who were carrying firearms and itching for fights. At least three of them have previous felony convictions."

"Absalom sure knew how to pick his posse," she said, frustrated and disappointed.

"I guess if you're looking for guys who will do anything you want, you find men who have already broken the law in just about every way imaginable. Auto theft. Drug running. Assault with a deadly weapon. Simple assault. Armed robbery."

"Wow, that's quite a list."

"It is, and I'm wondering where he met all the low-life thugs."

"Prison?"

"We checked. His record is clean. Nothing in his past that should have put him in the path of so many criminals."

"Then, it doesn't make sense that so many are working for him."

"None of this makes sense." He nudged her backward until she was in the room again.

She sat on the mattress, heart thudding, mind humming as she tried to put all the pieces together. Absalom. A bunch of criminals. A compound out in the middle of nowhere that pretended to be a posh resort.

"I wonder what he's hiding out there?" she murmured, reaching for a cup of water that sat on a table beside.

He lifted it for her, held it to her lips.

"The police plan to find out. They've closed the place down, sent all the guests home, and they're combing through every cabin, every yurt and every outbuilding."

"What about the residents? Are they still there?"

"I don't know."

"They're nice people, Radley. And they have nowhere else to go. That's their home. If they're forced to leave, they'll have nothing."

"I'll call Officer Wallace and ask him, if that'll make you feel better," he offered as he set the cup back on the table.

She shook her head. "Let's go out there instead. See for ourselves, make sure the crime scenes are processed properly."

"Damien Wallace seems like a nice enough guy, but I doubt he's going to be happy to have us hanging around critiquing his work or the work of the Vermont State Crime Lab."

She'd known that.

She'd just been hoping Radley would be curious enough to ignore protocol and take her back to the compound.

Apparently, he wasn't.

"It was just a thought." She got up from the bed and paced across the room, restless because she was in the hospital and because she still didn't know what was going on. "Have you been able to reach Wren? Maybe she'll have some insight into things."

"She and Henry Miller are on the way here."

"Henry? It's Friday, isn't it?" She'd seen the calendar on the receptionist's desk when she'd been checked in.

"Early Saturday morning, if you want to be technical."

"Either way, I'm surprised Henry agreed to come. He never works on weekends." A widower whose wife had been the victim of a drive-by shooting a month before their twin daughters were due, he'd said goodbye to his wife and hello to his children on the same day.

She hadn't known him then, but she'd heard people whispering about how devastated he'd been, about the fact that he'd almost quit the agency and probably would have if Wren hadn't offered him extended leave and a chance to return whenever he was ready. Six months later, he'd finally returned.

From what Honor had heard, he hadn't worked a weekend since.

During the week, he arrived at the office after he dropped the girls off at his parents' place. He sometimes worked late hours, and his mother would bring them home, tuck them into bed and wait until his return. The weekends, though, were sacred, set aside for the girls, for church, for catching up on the things he got behind on during the week. He'd told Honor that once when they'd both been taking the elevator to the lobby early one Friday evening.

"His in-laws took the twins on a Disney cruise to celebrate their fifth birthday. They'll be gone until late Sunday night."

"He should have enjoyed his quiet house and stayed far away from this mess."

"You sound disgusted."

"I am. Absalom should already be behind bars. The state police should have been out at the compound with a search warrant in hand within a half hour of Wren calling in the request for assistance."

"Even a half hour probably would have been too long, Honor. Absalom was probably gone before we escaped."

"I shot him full of a sedative, remember?"

"And he had plenty of followers who probably knew how to dose him with something that would wake him up."

"You're being reasonable, Radley. I appreciate that, but I'm not happy about any of this."

"I might have some information that will brighten your mood," he said, a slight smile softening the hard angles of his face.

"What?"

"I asked Wren to see if she could get information on the training seminar Mary Alice is attending. She put in some calls, asked around, spoke to some people who keep tabs on local cults. There is a training facility in Saugus. Housed in an old Victorian. Nice big sign out in front promising spiritual awakening to anyone who enters. Wren accessed the sales records. Guess who the owner is?"

"Absalom Winslow? You found Mary Alice!" she nearly shouted, throwing her arms around him just like she would have a friend or sibling. Just like she'd once done when she was working on difficult projects with groups of fellow tech geeks. Friendly excitement. That was all she meant to convey, but his arms slipped around her waist. She caught a whiff of coffee and soap, felt herself leaning in closer, enjoying the warmth of his body, the gentleness of his touch.

She was so surprised by that, so shocked, she was frozen in place. Not sure if she should back away, finish the hug, pretend nothing had happened.

His grip tightened, he tugged her closer, and then, just as quickly, stepped away.

"That was stupid. I'm sorry," she managed to say, embarrassed because she'd thrown herself into the arms of a coworker, a fellow member of the Special Crimes Unit, a guy she'd be seeing five days a week for a long time. Unless one of them quit.

And she didn't think either of them planned to do that.

"What's stupid about it?" he asked.

"We're coworkers. Not friends," she replied.

"Interesting," he responded, studying her face, his eyes dark and unreadable.

"What?"

"I didn't think there was a rule against being both."

"Of course, there isn't. It's just..."

"What?"

"Friendship sometimes leads to other things."

"Sometimes it doesn't."

"Right." Her cheeks were hot and that frustrated her. She didn't usually get flustered.

"So, how about we don't worry about where our friendship could lead and just allow ourselves to be friends?"

"Right. Of course. Sure," she said, still fumbling and flustered.

He smiled. Gently. Easily. As if maybe he'd felt exactly what she had when they'd hugged and was just as confused.

"We'll worry about everything else later," he continued.

"Everything else?" she asked, but he chucked her under the chin, a friendly gesture that shouldn't have made her heart swoon.

But, it did.

Like some lovelorn heroine of a romance novel.

And then he walked out of the room, closed the door and left her standing there with her cheeks hot and her pulse racing.

"Idiot," she muttered. "You are *not* attracted to Radley Tumberg. You are not going to spend another second thinking about what would happen if you were, and he was. You aren't!"

She walked to the window, pulled open the heavy curtains and looked outside. Rain was still pouring from the sky, splattering into the parking lot below. There weren't many cars there. Just a few parked haphazardly. Some close to the building. Some farther. She didn't see Radley's truck, but then, she wasn't sure she was facing the emergency room lot where he'd parked it.

A light flashed, a quick burst coming from the edge of the lot.

She was down before her brain could register what she'd seen, instinct kicking in before thoughts could form.

The window exploded, glass showering down on her, but she was already moving, crawling across the room, jumping up to flick off the light as the door flew open and Radley raced in.

Cold air and rain swept into the room, curtains billowing away from the shattered window. Absalom's work. Radley knew it, and he wanted to go after the guy before he had a chance to escape.

"Are you okay?" he asked, lifting Honor off her feet as he hurried her from the room.

"I think so." She brushed bits of glass from her arm, her eyes deep blue in the corridor's harsh light. "But I'm sure Absalom would be happy if I wasn't."

"Did you see him?"

"All I saw was a flash of light across the parking lot," she replied, the words brusque.

"You shouldn't have been near the window," he said, the words slipping out because she could have been killed. One bullet and good aim. That was all it would have taken.

"No need to rub salt in the open wound," she replied without heat. "I'm well aware of how stupid it was to pull back the curtains and stand there like a sitting duck waiting to be shot."

"Stand like a sitting duck?" he asked, because they were both tense, frustrated and angry about what had happened, and he needed to lighten the mood and clear their minds so that they could think through their options.

She smiled. "Funny guy, but I'm still frustrated with myself. I know better."

"You're okay. That's what matters."

"What matters is catching Absalom," she responded, taking a step toward the room.

He pulled her up short, his fingers loose around her wrist. "I am pretty certain we just established that you should stay away from the window."

"Right. He was across the parking lot. If we hurry, we might be able to catch him."

"*We're* not doing anything," he replied as a nurse and security guard raced toward them.

"Everyone okay here?" the guard asked, his attention on the open door to the room.

"You need to call the police and get someone outside. You've got an active shooter nearby," Radley replied. He wanted to run outside himself, search the rain-soaked landscape until he found Absalom, but he couldn't leave Honor with a security guard who wasn't armed and looked like he might still be in high school.

"I've already done both, sir," the young man said. "The officer who escorted you here was giving our team instructions on keeping the building secure." He blushed, apparently realizing the irony of what he was saying. "He's already heading outside and has called for backup."

"We should join him," Honor said, grabbing her IV pole and marching to the bank of elevators. She looked like she meant business. Even with glass glittering in her hair and specks of blood on her cheeks, an IV pole in one hand and a catheter in her arm, she looked like a woman on a mission. One who had no intention of being stopped.

"Wren and Henry should be here soon. When they arrive, I'll find Officer Wallace and have him update me on what he's discovered. For now, it's best if we both stay here," he said, moving into place beside her. Trying not to think about how it had felt when she'd thrown herself into his arms. As if everything that had ever been wrong was suddenly right. He'd stepped back, because the feeling had surprised him.

Now he was close again. Moving into her space, because he was afraid for her.

"I'm not going to hide, Radley," she said. "That's not the way I work."

She pulled at the tape covering the IV catheter and needle, and he had the feeling she was going to remove it, yank out the needle and go.

"Maybe not, but I promised your grandmother I'd bring you home. I didn't mean in a body bag."

She met his eyes. "I'm not going out there to let him kill me. I'm going so that he'll think he has the chance."

"You're talking about using yourself as bait?"

"Do you have a better idea?"

"Only about three dozen," he replied, frustrated with her persistence, and maybe a little impressed by it.

Because he wanted Absalom, too, and Honor was the surefire way to get him.

"Okay. Throw one at me. If it's a good one, I'll agree to cower in a room while you go off and do the he-man thing."

"He-man?"

"The hero running to the rescue? Facing all the obstacles. Doing the hard work while the poor insipid woman twiddles her thumbs and prays for help?"

"You're a lot of things, Honor. Insipid isn't one of them."

She looked up from the tape she'd been picking at, met his eyes, and he felt the same connection he had when she'd thrown her arms around him.

As if a tilting world had suddenly straightened and life made sense again.

"That's nice of you to say, Radley. And, since you think it, how about we go ahead and get this show on the road?" she responded as the elevator doors slid open.

"What show?" Wren Santino asked, stepping off the elevator, Henry Miller by her side. Both were tall, thin and muscular. Both moved with purpose and confidence. Wren carried a cup of coffee and had an oversized bag hanging from her shoulder. Despite the fact that it was after work hours and she'd left Boston in a hurry, she was dressed like the agent she was—dark pantsuit perfectly fitted, tailored shirt, jacket open and revealing flashes of her shoulder holster and firearm. As always, her hair was pulled back into a neat bun. If she wore makeup it was subtle enough not to be noticeable. If she didn't, her skin was nearly flawless, the shallow lines at the corner of her eyes the only hint that she was nearing her mid-thirties.

"We're discussing a plan to bring Absalom Winslow into custody," Honor responded.

"And, that would be what?" Wren asked, taking a sip of coffee, her gaze flitting from Honor to Radley and back again.

"Someone shot out the window in my room," Honor continued. "I believe it was Winslow, and I think if I go outside, we may be able to draw him closer to the building."

"You want to walk outside with an IV in your arm and play bait for a killer?" Wren raised a dark brow and shook her head. "I think we can come up with a better plan. Henry, would you mind escorting Honor to her room while Radley and I check the exterior of the building?"

"No problem," Henry responded.

"And, can you take this with you?" She pulled a gun holster from her bag and then handed the bag to him.

"I can do that, too," he agreed. Unlike Wren, he was dressed in civilian clothes. Well-worn jeans. A flannel shirt. Both faded and a little wrinkled. If Radley hadn't seen the guy in action, he'd have taken him for tech crew. He had that kind of vibe. Soft-spoken, quick to listen, slow to speak. Always hunkered over files, searching for details that might have been missed. He didn't waste time taking lunch breaks away from his desk. When he was in the office, he was in—completely focused and totally devoted to whatever case he was working on. When he was in the field, he was quick and decisive, but his ability to put people at ease, to make them trust him, was what put Radley to shame. Of all of the agents on the team, Henry was the one who could drag answers and information from the most reluctant of witnesses.

"Come on, Honor." Henry cupped her elbow. "Let's find a room that doesn't have a window blown out, and if you're up to it, you can tell me what you remember about your time at the Sanctuary." He was using the soothing tone Radley had heard him use with witnesses.

Honor didn't seem impressed.

"I'm not going to break, Henry. You don't have to talk to speak with me as if I might."

"You are one of the most unbreakable human-beings I've ever met," Henry responded, already leading her away.

"Now, you're trying to flatter me into compliance," Honor retorted, and Henry laughed.

For some reason, that made Radley want to follow, to stake a claim he had no right to.

He frowned.

"You don't look happy," Wren commented, and he met her eyes, realized she'd been watching him watch Honor walk away.

"A madman with a firearm is wandering free. Should I be?"

She smiled. "You have a firearm?"

"Yes."

"Holster?"

"No."

"I didn't think so." She handed him the holster. "Strap it on. I don't like my agents carrying firearms around in their waistbands."

He strapped on the holster, tucked the gun into it and nodded. "Let's go."

"And, hope he's still out there. It's interesting that he managed to find Honor here, isn't it?" she asked as pressed the elevator call button. "We're forty-five minutes from Absalom's compound."

"True, but Honor was injured. He knew that. He probably assumed we'd go get treatment for the injuries."

"There are medical centers between Sunrise Spiritual Sanctuary and Hartford. Three of them. All of them are open twenty-four hours. There's also a small hospital ten miles east of here. Close enough that you might have chosen to go there."

True. All of it.

That was one of the things he liked about Wren. She was clear-thinking, smart and focused.

"So, how'd he wind up here?" she continued as they stepped onto the elevator and the doors closed. "And how did he happen to see her standing in the window? This building is three stories tall, and she said he was across the parking lot."

"Those are good questions."

"Let's find the answers, find the perp and put him away where he belongs."

The elevator doors opened again, and she led the way through the lobby and outside.

They crossed the parking lot together, the sound of radios ringing through the predawn darkness. Police and security guards were moving between sparsely parked cars, searching for the perpetrator.

They wouldn't find him.

Absalom wasn't stupid.

He'd found his way here, and he planned to accomplish his goal. Wren stopped at the edge of the lot, turning to look at the building.

Honor's room was three stories up, the curtains billowing out of the open window. Someone had turned on the light, and he could see a man standing with his back to the shattered glass.

"It's a clear view," he said.

"Yes, but he would have had to know what room to look at. I can't see who's standing in that window. Or, in any of the other ones."

"Someone fed him information," Radley muttered, disgusted by the thought.

"I wonder if he has any connections in the police department? We'll do some digging and find out. For now, we need to stop the outflow of information."

"It will be easier to do that when we're on our own turf."

"I agree," Wren said, still staring at the blown-out window. "I've asked the state police to dust for prints in Absalom's home. Specifically, his bathroom. His name isn't in the system, but I have a feeling he hasn't always been on the right side of the law. He was probably the last person to touch the sink and shower faucets. If he left clear prints, we might get a match to another name."

"Prints would be good. Finding him would better."

"Right," she agreed.

Rain was still falling, splashing in puddles and seeping into cracked asphalt. There were no bullet casing that Radley could see, but someone had stuck a small flag in the grass nearby. He walked to it, eyed a depression in the soil next to the flag.

"It looks like an officer has been here."

"And, flagged that for an evidence team." Wren pulled out a Maglite and aimed it at the spot. "Someone was standing here for long enough to leave an impression." The light swept across the grassy expanse that stretched from the asphalt to a line of trees. "Look." She focused the light on a barren spot, the muddy earth tamped down by what looked like the heel of a shoe.

"He came through the trees," Radley said. And, he'd left through them. Probably disappearing into the shadows of the forest before the first police officer ran across the parking lot.

Radley walked to the patch of mud, crouching near it, water dripping down his chin and splashing onto the ground. "It looks like a boot."

"It's definitely not a sandal," Wren commented.

"Sandal?"

"I figured the leader of a spiritual sanctuary might be into sandals and robes."

"His paramilitary guards weren't."

"So, maybe he was driven here by one of his devoted followers. He certainly didn't walk to the hospital."

"But, he walked through those trees to get to it. And, he could still be walking. How about we go take a look?" he suggested, already walking toward the trees.

This he knew how to do.

Hunt down bad guys. Bring them in. Assure their victims' safety, sanity, peace of mind.

No matter how much he wanted to, he couldn't change the past.

Not his. Certainly not anyone else's.

But, he could change the future.

He could make it easier for those who'd suffered to move forward and live free of fear by finding the people who'd abused, hurt, taken advantage of them.

He couldn't wipe out memories or make the pain of loss disappear, but he could make certain that justice was done, that victims had closure, that one less monster was loose on the world.

He'd do that now, and then he'd do what he'd promised Dotty. He'd bring Honor home.

EIGHT

An hour passed.

Two.

Honor sat in a chair, back to the wall, a file folder in her lap. Henry had handed it to her as soon as they'd found a safe room, telling her that Wren had gathered information about The Sanctuary and wanted her to read it.

She suspected they'd both wanted her occupied.

She didn't do well sitting around waiting. She liked action. Even if that action was finding her way through computer systems and following cyber-trails.

So, she'd read the file through six times, attempting to find something that would help her understand what had happened to Mary Alice. Knowing that should be the key to figuring out Absalom's motives.

There was nothing.

Just pages of information about the way Absalom's community worked. His philosophy. His religion. His dogma. General estimates of the size of his followers, the numbers and demographics. Risk assessment.

None of it pointed at murder as high on Absalom's agenda.

But he'd tried to kill her.

To keep Mary Alice from leaving?

Maybe, but murder was a huge risk, and Absalom seemed risk averse. If he'd wanted Honor dead, he could have killed her while she was unconscious in the yurt. He'd let her live, and she could only assume that was because he'd wanted her to die naturally, make her death look like a tragic result of the accident and resulting infection.

She shuddered, eying the IV bag, the fluid still dripping into her arm. She'd asked to have it removed. So far, the request hadn't been granted.

"Staring at it won't make it disappear," Henry said, not looking up from a book he was reading.

He was just a few feet away, sitting to the right of the door. Facing the window even though heavy drapes covered it. He hadn't left the room since they'd entered, hadn't used his phone, hadn't tried to contact Wren or Radley.

Honor was chomping at the bit to do both.

"I don't know how you can be so calm," she muttered, setting the file on the bed beside her.

"I'm not the one who was shot at," he replied, closing the book and meeting her eyes. He had dark eyes, fair skin, black hair with a hint of gray at the temple. She'd seen photos of his daughters on his desk at work, both of them black-haired pixies with big blue eyes.

"Your wife must have had blue eyes," she said without meaning to. His smile remained, but something shifted in his eyes, and she knew she'd crossed a professional line.

"I'm sorry. That's really none of my business," she said hurriedly.

"It's okay." He brushed off her apology. "She did have blue eyes. The girls inherited them. I guess you've seen the pictures I keep on my desk."

"Yes, but like I said, not my business. Sorry. Again."

"You apologize a lot, Honor."

"I do?"

"It's something I've noticed about you when you're presenting your findings to the team. It always surprised me, because you are thorough and your presentations are well-organized and interesting."

"I…have no idea how to respond to that," she admitted. She didn't think she was more prone to apology than anyone else, but she'd never listened to one of her presentations. She knew she'd spent a lot of her adolescent years apologizing for bumping into people, knocking things over, getting in the way. Her head had always been filled with questions, her mind teeming with thoughts. Even then, she'd been caught up in the cyber world, losing herself in technology because it had been easier to understand than her peers.

"It's just an observation," he replied, setting the book on a table and leaning forward, his elbows on his knees. "There's no need to respond. I only noticed because my wife used to apologize all the time. She was a programmer, her head wrapped up in all kinds of things I couldn't understand. I guess I just noticed your habit, because she had the same one. I wondered if it was something to do with being in the computer industry."

"For me, it's more to do with being in my own head too much. I tend to knock things over and bump into people unintentionally," she admitted, and he smiled.

"My wife did, too."

"I doubt she was any match for me. I must have broken twenty glasses a year when I was a kid. It drove my uncle crazy."

"Bennett Remington, right?" he asked, and

she nodded, not surprised that he knew her uncle's name.

"He's good at what he does," Henry commented, not even a hint of judgment in his face or his tone.

"Very."

"How does he feel about what you do?"

"My father was a police officer, so my career path seemed like a natural choice. I'm sure my uncle would agree," she said, because she had no idea how Bennett felt about what she did. He hadn't been involved in helping her choose the right college or the right career path. As a matter of fact, since she'd graduated high school, he'd mostly stayed out of her life.

"But, you don't know?"

"No, I don't."

He nodded, watching her with a steady gaze that made her wonder what he was seeing. "What?" she finally asked, and he shrugged.

"Just curious."

"About?"

"A man who doesn't have any say in the life of the woman he helped raise."

"Bennett has a busy high-stress career. He doesn't have time to worry about other people."

"I'd hate for my girls to say that about me one day," he commented, and she shrugged.

"Because you care about your daughters. Bennett cares about himself."

The phone beside the bed rang, and she jumped about a foot, her heart nearly leaping from her chest.

"Who could that be?" she asked, as if Henry could possibly know.

He lifted the receiver, pressed it to his ear.

"Hello?" He waited, nodded. "Yes, she is. Can I ask who's calling?" He listened, put his hand over the mouthpiece. "It's Mary Alice Stevenson."

She nearly snatched the phone from his hands, her grip clumsy because of the bandages, her heart still pounding riotously as she pressed it to her ear. "Hello?"

"Honor?" Mary Alice said.

"Yes! I can't believe it's you! I've been trying to reach you for weeks!" she nearly shouted, her voice trembling with relief and fear and joy.

"I know. I'm sorry. I should never have run away from my problems. I should have just sat down and talked to you and my parents."

"What's going on, Mary Alice? Whatever it is, I'll help you find a way out of it."

"It's complicated and stupid. Just a dumb mistake I should have known better than to make."

"Are you at home?" Honor jabbed the nurse's

call button on the bed rail. She was getting the IV out, she was finding a ride and she was going to wherever Mary Alice was.

"No, I'm calling from a training center in Saugus. It's called—"

"The Spiritual Awakening Learning Center?"

"How did you know?"

"I told you, I've been trying to track you down. Your parents were worried when you said you weren't returning from your retreat. They asked me to check it out."

"I wish they hadn't gotten you involved."

"We grew up together. We're best friends. Of course they got me involved." She jabbed the call button again. "And, of course, I came looking for you. Even though you've barely spoken to me since you called off your wedding."

"I'm sorry about that. I really am."

"I don't need an apology. I just want to know that you're all right."

"I am, and I'll explain everything when we see each other, okay? I know it won't make things better, but I owe you that."

"We'll be seeing each other as soon as I can hitch a ride to Saugus. I should be there in a few hours. Stay there until I arrive, okay?"

"I don't have a choice. The FBI raided the

facility a few hours ago. They're keeping us all until we've been questioned."

"Is that why you called?" Honor asked, some of her excitement fading. She'd hoped that Mary Alice had reached out because she'd missed their friendship.

"No! I've been wanting to call, but they take everything when you arrive, and the only phone in this place is in a locked office. I've been trying to get to it for a week. This has been my first chance. I called my parents, and they told me you'd been hospitalized. Your Uncle Bennett called Dotty to let her know, and she called the church prayer chain. You know how that works."

"Yes. I do."

"My parents called Bennett, and he was able to tell them what hospital you'd been admitted to. I'm so sorry, Honor. This is all my fault."

"Of course, it's not. I chose to come out here." She reached for the button again, and Henry grabbed her wrist, his grip loose and gentle.

"I don't think they'll appreciate you hitting that button again," he said.

Right. They wouldn't, and she didn't want to irritate the people she was hoping would hurry up and get to the room.

"I'll make this up to you, Honor. I will.

You're the best friend I've ever had, and I don't know why I didn't just come to you at the beginning of all this."

"Of all what?" she asked.

"I've got to go. Someone else wants to use the phone. I love you, sweetie." She disconnected, and Honor stood with the phone still pressed to her ear, tethered by the IV pole and wondering just what her friend had been hiding.

"If you're thinking of making a run for the door," Henry said quietly. "Don't. I'd feel compelled to stop you, and I don't want there to be any hard feelings between us because of it."

"Why would you think I would make a run for it?"

"Because you're staring at the door and you look ready to sprint."

"Ready, maybe. But probably not prepared to do it." She tried to smile, easing back into the chair and telling herself to relax. There was nothing she could do until the IV was removed.

Except sit and fret about things she couldn't change.

Like the fact that Mary Alice was in Saugus, and she wasn't.

"I hope she's okay," she murmured, picking at the tape on her arm again, and telling herself not to push the nurse's call button for the third or fourth or fifth time.

"Will it make you feel better if I make a few phone calls? See if I can get an agent involved in keeping an eye on her?" he asked, pulling a phone from his pocket.

"That sounds an awful lot like getting someone to spy on her."

"And?"

"We're best friends. It doesn't seem right to sic the FBI on her. Besides, I trust her to do what she said she would."

"You can't have it both ways, Honor."

"What do you mean?"

"You can't trust her to do what she told you and worry about her not doing it at the same time."

She thought about that for a minute.

Decided he was wrong, because she felt both those things—certain Mary Alice would stay at the facility and concerned that she wouldn't.

"What may be impossible for other people has apparently proven very possible for me," she finally said, and he grinned.

"I keep telling my daughters nothing is impossible if you believe. I guess you've just proven it. Wait here, I'll find a nurse. Since, I can see that you're almost overwhelmingly tempted to push that button again."

"Thanks, Henry."

"No problem." He stepped out of the room, closing the door quietly behind him.

And, she was alone, staring at the tape, wondering if she could pull out the IV without passing out.

She'd never been super wimpy about blood.

Then again, she'd never been overly brave about it either.

But, if she could get the IV out, she'd be one step closer to leaving the hospital and getting to Saugus.

She was about to yank the tape off when the door swung open.

She expected Henry, and she didn't bother looking up. She'd set her course, and she planned to follow through.

On three, she told herself.

One.

Two.

"Don't even think about it," Radley said, his voice so surprising she screamed. Only it sounded more like the high-pitched squeal Wilbur used when he wanted out of his pen. Maybe a little more frantic and a whole lot louder.

"You scared me half to death," she gasped, her hand flying to her chest, because she was certain her heart was going to jump out of it.

"*I* scared *you*? You're the one who's trying to pull a needle out of your vein." He crossed the room, pressed the tape back into place. "The nurse will be here in a minute. She'll take this out, and then we're hitting the road."

Water dripped down his face, splashing onto the floor at his feet. He was soaked to the skin, his lips nearly blue from cold, and she forgot about Mary Alice, the IV, the need to hurry.

"You're freezing. You shouldn't have stayed out there so long," she chided, grabbing a blanket and trying to toss it around his shoulders. The bandages and IV got in the way, but she finally managed, pulling the edges together in front of his chest and pressing them into his hand. "Hold this. I'll get a towel from the bathroom."

"Don't bother. Some of Officer Wallace's men found my duffel and your backpack at The Sanctuary. They're bringing them here. I'll dry off and change when they arrive."

She ignored him, grabbing a towel and returning to his side. She used it to dab at his hair and his cheeks, wipe water from the back of his neck. His skin was cold to the touch, and if her hands hadn't been bandaged, she'd have rubbed warmth into his arms and shoulders.

"Honor, stop," he said so quietly she almost didn't hear. He took the towel from her hands to emphasize the point, dropping it on the table, his expression grim and hard.

"What's wrong? Did you find Absalom? Was Wren hurt? What aren't you telling me?" she asked, searching his eyes, trying to find answers there.

"We didn't find him, Wren is fine, and I've told you everything I know."

"Then what's going on?"

"I don't like this. Any of it," he muttered. "Somehow Absalom showed up at this hospital, found your room and fired a shot into it. He had to have been told you were here. Had to have been given your room number."

"Or, he just chanced into both. There aren't a lot of hospitals around here, and he could have driven to several before he came here," she suggested, but he was right. She knew it, had known it from the moment she'd seen the flash of light and heard the shattering glass.

"You don't believe that, Honor."

"No, I don't, but the only other option is that someone is feeding him information. I hate to think of any of Officer Wallace's men being dirty."

"They're not."

"You've already checked into it?"

"He pulled phone records before I asked, because he was thinking the same thing. He has twenty officers, and none of them were in contact with Absalom or anyone affiliated with The Sanctuary."

"He could be responsible," she offered.

He shook his head. "He pulled his phone records, too, because he knew we'd want to see them."

"Okay," she said, sorting through the facts, trying to move her way from point A to point C without stopping at point B, because that was the point that would sit directly over someone she knew, and she couldn't think of anyone who'd have Absalom's contact information except…

"She would never do that to me," she said.

She didn't say the name.

She didn't need to.

He'd sorted through the same facts and had made the same connections.

"I know Mary Alice is your friend, Honor, but Wren called her parents to let them know she'd been located. They said they'd already spoken to their daughter. Mary Alice had called them an hour before agents arrived at the training center, said she missed all of you and that she'd been trying to call you to let you know she was okay. They'd heard about your hospitalization and had gotten the room number from Bennett, so that they could send you flowers. They gave her the hospital name and the room number. I called to confirm that five minutes ago."

"That's circumstantial evidence at best," she protested, but the words rang hollow, because everything he was saying all made sense.

"Honor?" He touched her chin, urged her to look into his eyes. "It's possible we're reading the situation wrong, but Wren has asked agents to bring Mary Alice in for questioning. She's agreed to allow you to be there if you want."

"What I want," she said, turning away, because she didn't want him to see the tears in her eyes, "is to get this IV out of my arm."

"Avoiding the issue isn't going to make it go away," he cautioned.

He might be right, but at that moment she didn't care.

She had no desire to discuss Mary Alice, Absalom, The Sanctuary. All she wanted was to be left alone.

"I need…to wash my face." She walked into the bathroom, closed the door with a quiet snap that wasn't nearly as satisfying as slamming it would have been.

He knocked. Of course, because that was how he was at work—persistent, willing to follow every lead, in the office early every day of the week, staying late. Writing reports, doing research, making calls and then moving out into the world again, going after the worst kind of pond scum, the foulest human beings.

"Honor? It's going to be hard to wash your face with your hands bandaged," he called.

"I'll manage," she responded, turning on the water and watching as it poured into the sink.

He thought about knocking again.

He almost did, but Wren walked into the room.

"How'd it go?" she asked, her gaze on the closed bathroom door.

"About as horribly as we expected." Which was why he'd wanted Wren or Henry to break the news to Honor. He wasn't cut out for this kind of thing. He didn't know how to take the sting out of his words, make situations seem less bleak than they were.

Pretend things that weren't true.

He'd wanted to, though. He'd looked into Honor's eyes, he'd known how much she was hurting and he'd wanted to agree that Mary Alice hadn't betrayed her, that their friendship was everything she'd believed it to be.

He'd wanted to, but he couldn't.

The truth mattered. Always. Even when it hurt people he cared about.

"In that case, I'll assume you didn't get

to ask her why Mary Alice might want her harmed," Wren said, grabbing her bag from the corner where Henry had left it.

The bathroom door flew open, and Honor stood on the threshold, face pale, eyes blazing. "She wouldn't."

"You're upset," Wren said. "Rightfully so."

"I'm not upset," Honor replied, her voice cold and devoid of emotion. "I'm just making my opinion known. Mary Alice wouldn't kill a fly that landed in her jam. When she was in kindergarten, she accidentally stepped on an ant, and she cried because it died."

"People change, Honor. And sometimes they don't. Sometimes, they make poor choices and big mistakes. Good people sometimes do bad things. You've been in this business long enough to know that," Wren replied, shuffling together papers that had been left on a table, tucking them into a manila folder and dropping it into the bag.

"That's the angle you have to take, Wren, because you're leading the case, but I'm on medical leave. I don't have to think like a federal agent. Right now, I'm choosing to think like a friend."

"I understand," Wren said calmly. "I'd feel the same if I were in your situation. I want you to know that."

"I appreciate it, but it doesn't help."

"I understand that, too."

A nurse stepped into the room, young and fresh-faced, a broad smile on her face. Her gaze darted from person to person, and the smile faded.

"I'm sorry for interrupting. I'll come back in a few minutes," she said.

"Wait," Honor said. "I've decided to head home. I'd like the IV removed."

"The doctor feels it's best if you stay for at least twenty-four hours, Ms. Remington."

"I know, but I have an elderly grandmother who hasn't seen me in two weeks. She's worried sick, and that's making me worry. I'm sure you understand." She smiled, and Radley could almost believe she wasn't upset. Almost.

"I have two," the nurse replied, stepping further into the room. "They both excel at worrying about me."

"Then you *do* understand. Dotty won't sleep a wink until I'm safely home, and I won't sleep until she does. I know the doctor prefers me to stay, but I *can* legally discharge myself."

"That's true."

"And I have a wonderful medical team in Boston."

"I love Boston," the nurse gushed, pulling gloves from a container hanging on the wall.

"I'm hoping to get a job in the city once I have some experience under my belt."

"You could probably get one now," Honor replied, keeping up the cheerful chatter as the nurse opened cupboards, took out gauze and bright-colored wrap and removed the IV.

As soon as she left the room, Honor fell silent, all the faux cheerfulness falling away.

"Just so you know," she said quietly, "just because I don't want to believe that Mary Alice is involved doesn't mean I can't see why you both would. It makes a terrible kind of sense. All of it. But I'm not ready to discuss it. For now, I'll just say I have no idea why Mary Alice would want to harm me, and I'll leave it at that."

She sounded tired and a little defeated, but in that moment, Radley had as much respect for her as he'd ever had for anyone. It took strength to push aside emotion and look at things through clear lenses. It took guts to admit that something painful could be the truth.

He wanted to tell her that, but a police officer arrived with their bags, and Wren offered to get everyone a cup of coffee for the road. Henry returned, and the opportunity was lost in the hubbub of planning their trip back to Boston.

With Absalom still on the loose, they had to be meticulous in their attention to detail. Every road, every stop. All the places where they could be ambushed or preyed upon pinpointed and highlighted.

He changed clothes when Wren returned, pulling the holster back into place, double-checking the gun. He'd prefer his own firearm, but this was better than nothing.

When he stepped out of the bathroom, Wren was at the door, bag slung over her shoulder, gaze sharp.

"Everyone ready?" she asked. "Let's head out."

She opened the door, hesitated. "Do you smell that?"

"No," he began to say, but the scent of something drifted into the room. Dark and musty, acrid and harsh.

"Yes," he corrected.

"Smoke? If that's what it is, why isn't the alarm sounding?" Henry asked, his hand on Honor's arm.

As if his words had conjured it, a shrill alarm sounded, the high-pitched scream chilling Radley's blood.

He knew what it meant, what it heralded.

Absalom was somewhere nearby, waiting for an opportunity to strike.

NINE

She should have been terrified, but Honor had three of the best federal agents she knew playing bodyguard, and mostly, she just felt tired. She wanted to leave the shrieking alarm, the hospital, the beautiful state of Vermont. She wanted to go home.

Not to the cute apartment she rented in downtown Boston.

Home to the farm. To the wide fields and fenced pastures. To the barn that she'd painted brick red the previous year. She wanted to sit in Dotty's kitchen, sipping coffee and eating cookies from a plate piled high with them.

And she wanted to forget that her best friend might have betrayed her.

Why?

That was the question that filled her mind, and it seemed to be chasing everything else from her thoughts. She barely cared about the smoke billowing into the room, or Henry's tight grip on her arm.

She did care about survival, though, and when Wren sprinted to her side and hollered, "Out into the hall. We'll take the nearest stairs. He won't know which room you're in, and so he'll either be in the lobby or outside. Stick close to Henry. Radley and I will take care of the rest."

She sprinted into the hall, something niggling at the back of her mind, a worry she chalked up to the screaming siren, the smoke streaming up from the floor, her own nervous energy. She knew her team members could handle the situation. She knew they'd handled worse, but still…

She couldn't shake the feeling that something was off.

Henry guided her past nurses who were running into rooms. The hospital was small as hospitals went, but it served a large community. She prayed that the fire was contained, that no one was hurt, because if anyone died, she'd blame herself.

She'd brought Absalom here.

She kept pace with Henry, staying just a few steps behind Wren and Radley. They reached the stairwell, stopped at the door.

Radley turned, motioning for them to wait

while he and Wren entered the stairwell. He glanced through the small window in the door, searching the area beyond. Before he could open it, the siren shut off midscream, the sudden silence deafening.

A nurse hurried through the corridor, offering a wane smile. "Everything is okay. It was just a small trash fire in a bathroom. You can go back to your room," she said as she passed.

"Thoughts?" Wren asked, her gaze focused on Radley.

He didn't look like the man in the yurt—the one who'd held water to her lips, supported her as she tried to sit, the one who'd smiled, chuckled, helped her make it through acres of forest when it would have been easier to go on ahead.

He looked hard. Dangerous. Angry.

"It was him. I don't need proof to know that."

"Then, we stay on our guard and move out the way we planned. Down to the basement. Out the service door. We'll make sure the stairwell is secure," Wren said, opening the door and stepping across the threshold. "You two stay here until I give you the signal. I feel confident he's waiting for us to emerge from the building, but let's play it safe anyway."

And there it was again, the gnawing worry at the back of Honor's mind, a woodpecker tapping at her brain. Something was wrong, but she couldn't figure out what.

"What's wrong?" Radley asked, somehow sensing what she hadn't dared share. She worked in front of computers. She followed cyber trails. She did not run through the woods being chased by bad guys, track down villains, set traps or snares to bring in monsters. If her coworkers felt confident in the plan, she should too.

"Nothing," she said, because she still couldn't put her finger on the problem.

"Something," he responded, glancing at the stairwell door. "Would you mind going with Wren, Henry? I'll stay here."

"It's not part of the plan, but I'm not going to argue, as long as we get this done." Henry stepped into the stairwell, and it was just the two of them, looking into each other's eyes.

"Tell me what's wrong," he said.

"I don't know. Just…a feeling."

"About?"

"Absalom. Like I should know something, but don't." She frowned. "That makes no sense."

"It makes as much sense as anything else that has happened the past few hours." His phone buzzed, and he frowned. "That's the signal. The stairwell is clear."

"Then we'd better go," she said with more

confidence than she felt, her mind still trying to work the problem out, the constant tap-tap-tapping in her brain like the clack of computer keys when she was writing code. She knew how to manipulate information. She knew how to go in through back doors. She'd been an ace student at MIT, earning her master's degree a year after she'd gotten her bachelor's degree. She should be able to figure this out.

He opened the door, stepping in ahead of her while her brain clicked along, snapping bits and pieces of information into place, slowly at first, then faster and faster.

"She called me," she said, her words echoing in the stairwell as she followed him onto the stairs.

"Who?"

"Mary Alice. She called the hospital."

"And?"

"The lines are direct. If you have the room number, you don't have to go through the operator. She'd have called the first room I was in because that's the room number everyone associated me with. When she didn't reach me, she'd have called the information line and asked for my room number."

He swung toward her, apparently processing the information a lot more quickly than she had. She could see understanding in his eyes, knew that he was thinking what she should have been before they'd ever walked out of the room. *If* Mary Alice had given Absalom her room number the first time, she could just as easily have done it again.

The knowledge hurt. Physically. Pulsing in the region of her heart, because for as long as they'd known each other, she and Mary Alice had been each other's greatest cheerleaders and closest confidants.

At least, Honor *thought* they'd been.

"This doesn't mean I think she gave him my room number," she said, but Radley was already sprinting up the stairs, grabbing her arm, pulling her in the opposite direction of where they were supposed to go.

In years to come, she thought she'd remember that more than anything—the way Radley immediately assessed the situation, made a decision and acted on it. There'd been no hesitation. No checking with Wren or Henry. He'd known what needed to be done, and he was doing it.

They passed the third-floor landing, bounded onto a narrower track of steps. This one led to a door that she thought would open to the roof. A huge sign was plastered across the front—*Emergency Exit Only!*

Somewhere below, a door flew open, banging against the wall. Her heart skipped a beat, raced forward again. Absalom was coming. She knew it. He'd been waiting for her to walk past the second-or first-floor door, planning to shoot her through the window, or open the door just as she passed. Either way, he'd planned for her to die.

She wanted to know why, but she wanted to live more than she wanted to stay and ask.

Radley's phone buzzed twice, and she was sure Wren and Henry were trying to contact him. He ignored it, shoving open the door and setting off an alarm that nearly pierced Honor's eardrums. It didn't seem to be enough to chase Absalom away. He was a floor down, and she could see him clearly. No longer wearing flowy white clothes, he looked like what he was—a drug-addicted thug, his face gaunt, his shirt hanging from a concave chest.

She caught just a glimpse of his dead eyes as Radley pulled her out into a small alcove and slammed the door.

There was nothing to block it. No way to keep it closed. A few feet away, metal rungs led to the rooftop.

"Come on," Radley lifted her onto them, gave her a gentle shove upward. "Climb!"

She did, scrambling up faster than she'd have ever believed possible, slipping on concrete as she reached the roof and clambered onto it.

There were several structures jutting up from the flat surface, and she thought she saw another alcove and the top edge of rungs like the ones she'd just climbed. There was more than one stairwell in the hospital. There had to be more than one entrance to the roof.

She sprinted in that direction, but Radley grabbed the back of her shirt, swinging her around in the opposite direction.

"That's where he'll think we're going, but doors like these lock from the inside. The only way to get back into the building is with a key," he said.

They darted around a thick chimney stack and raced across the roof, rain splattering around them. When they reached the four-foot wall that surrounded the roof, she knew they were trapped. A three-story fall in front of them. Death behind them.

"Radley," she said, grabbing his shoulders, staring straight into his eyes. "I just want you to know that I'm sorry. This is all my fault. I also want you to know that you really are an epic hero. If I were the kind of girl who was looking for one, you'd be exactly what I'd want to find."

The words slipped out, and she couldn't believe she'd said them. She hadn't even realized she'd been thinking them.

His mouth twitched but he didn't smile.

"Thank you," he responded, his lips brushing hers. Tenderly. Sweetly. The contact such a surprise, she almost forgot they were about to die.

He stepped back, climbed onto the wall and touched a metal rung that had been screwed into the cement.

"The fire escape is going to be slippery, but if we're careful, we can make it down. Be careful," he cautioned, extending his hand and helping her up.

"Fire escape?"

"I don't go anywhere that doesn't have an exit," he replied.

She looked down. Saw cars and pavement and puddles gleaming in the exterior lights. "I have told you I'm clumsy, right?"

"You're beautiful and accomplished, and I'm not going to let some insane cult leader shoot you," he replied. "Let's go. One rung at a time."

She had no choice.

She knew that.

If she refused, Absalom would find them.

Radley had a gun. She knew he was a good shot, but Absalom would shoot, too. And there was no guarantee of whom the bullet would hit.

She lowered herself over the side of the building, her feet finding the fire escape. It was metal attached to the cement and it wobbled as she put her weight on it.

"That's it. Easy." Radley said, a note of something in his voice. Worry, maybe. "Keep going, and you'll be down before you know it."

"Do I have a choice?" she muttered. She couldn't feel the metal through the thick bandages on her hands, and she wished she'd removed them. Too late now, she was clinging to the fire escape, moving like a snail. She didn't dare look up or down, didn't dare think about Absalom looming over the edge of the building, aiming his gun. She expected to feel the structure shake as Radley joined her.

She waited, taking one step after another, praying silently each time she moved a foot or hand.

It took her a minute to realize Radley wasn't coming. It took her another to realize he hadn't planned to.

He'd helped her escape, and he was going after Absalom.

Because, of course, if they were both on the fire escape and Absalom saw them, he'd shoot them down like skeets from the sky.

She should have thought about that *before* she'd started her descent.

She reached the third-story landing, which was nothing more than a wide metal grate. There was a door in the façade of the building, and she tried to open it. It was locked. She banged on it, hoping someone would hear. She needed to get inside, she needed to call for help.

Somewhere above her, a man was calling her name, the sound shivering up her spine and lodging in the base of her neck.

"Honor? I know you're up here. Don't be afraid. You are the chosen one. The living sacrifice."

She didn't like the sound of that, and she backed up against the door, hoping that if he looked down, he wouldn't see her.

"Your friend is gone. It's just the two of us now."

That sounded even worse, and she couldn't imagine it was true. There was no way that Absalom had silently taken Radley down. She knew that, but she still felt the urge to call Radley's name, make sure he was okay.

The metal shook, and she looked up, saw Absalom's face staring down at her. He was grinning, his eyes still dead and cold.

"There you are," he said, pointing a gun

straight at her head. "You've been way more trouble than you were worth."

She braced for the impact of the bullet, prayed Dotty would be okay without her, wondered whom she'd see first when she arrived in Heaven. Her parents? Her grandfather? Some distant relative she didn't remember meeting?

She thought she heard a man shout.

And then the world exploded.

The first bullet made contact, and Absalom went flying, the gun clattering across concrete as he slammed into the wall of the roof.

He was still alive. Radley hadn't taken a kill-shot, because any death was a tragedy. Even the death of a guy like this. Plus, he wanted to know what was going on, why Absalom was so determined to kill Honor. Someone was calling the shots, and he didn't think it was this scrawny, strung-out addict.

"Don't move," he warned as he approached.

Blood spurted from Absalom's wrist, the shattered bone showing through the skin. He'd probably lose the hand, and Radley couldn't find it in himself to be sorry.

"You shot me!" Absalom said, staring at his wrist as if he couldn't believe it had happened.

"I warned you to put the gun down."

"You shot me," he repeated, his left hand

shifting, something about the way he moved warning Radley seconds before he lunged. The blade of a knife flashed as it arched toward Radley's face. He jumped back, firing a shot that slammed into Absalom's gut. The guy just kept coming, head-butting him, left hand on Radley's wrist as he tried to wrest the gun away.

Radley shoved him back.

"On the ground. Belly down. Hands where I can see them!" he commanded, but Absalom was hopped up on something, his eyes wild, his mouth stretched in a wide grin.

"What's the matter? Can't handle what I'm bringing to the game?" He snatched his gun from the ground, and Radley would have fired, but Honor suddenly appeared, her head popping over the top of the wall. She climbed onto it and launched herself at Absalom, hitting him square in the back.

They both went flying, and then, Absalom was up again.

Radley shouted another command for him to stop, firing as the man whirled in his direction.

Absalom flew back, slamming into the wall, nearly falling over it before crumbling to the cement, bloody rainwater dripping onto the roof.

Radley kicked the gun away, his attention focused on making sure the threat was neutralized.

"Are you okay, Honor?" he called, not glancing in her direction. Whatever Absalom was on, it seemed to have muted his pain receptors. The guy's eyes were still wide open, his mouth twisted in a ghastly smile.

"I'm fine," she said. "Is he?"

"I'm the chosen one. I'll never die," Absalom replied.

"Maybe not," Radley replied, checking Absalom for weapons and then helping him lie prone. He shrugged out of his jacket and pressed it against the abdominal wound. There was one in the shoulder, too, bleeding sluggishly. He'd have called for help, but he could hear people racing out of the building, the metal rungs rattling as they climbed onto the roof.

"You're losing a lot of blood," Radley continued, feeling the pulse in Absalom's neck. It was thready and weak, his breathing shallow. "I hope whoever paid you to come after Honor made it worth dying for."

"Like I said, I'll never die," Absalom gasped, his eyes closing. "And I didn't take money. I was repaying a favor. One good deed deserves another, right?"

"A favor to who?" Radley asked as Wren and Henry raced toward them.

Absalom didn't respond.

Radley checked his pulse again. Still thready and weak.

Doctors and nurses were streaming across the wet roof, running with gurneys and medical supplies.

"Absalom?" Radley tried one more time. "Who were you doing the favor for?"

"My mom called me Kenny," Absalom said. "I never liked the name."

The medical team was there, and Radley moved back, letting them do what they could to save him.

It was still raining, blood mixing with the deluge and streaming across the cement. He could almost see Absalom's life streaming away with it.

"You did what you had to," Wren said, patting his arm. She knew what he was thinking, knew the sorrow mixed with relief that he felt. She'd stood in his shoes, held the weapon in her hand that had killed a person, and she understood in every way the weight of that responsibility.

"Just so you know," he responded. "This is my least favorite part of my job."

"I think it's all of ours. If it isn't, then we shouldn't be in this line of work."

He nodded, turning from the fallen man.

Honor was a few feet away, watching him, her expression somber.

"I'm sorry," she said. "I wish I could have saved you both."

"For the record," he replied, pulling her into his arms because she was shivering, "that was one of the most foolish things I've ever seen. It was also probably the bravest. Thanks for coming to my rescue."

"As if I did. You had things under control." She leaned into him just long enough for it to feel like she'd always been there—her head beneath his chin, her arms around his waist. Then she stepped back, brushing hair out of her face, the bandages on her hands slapping against her wrists. "I heard what he said about repaying a favor. Do you think he was talking about Mary Alice?"

"It would make sense."

"If we go with the hypothesis that she fed him information about my hospital room, it does. But, I still don't believe she did that."

"You don't *want* to believe it."

"I *can't* believe it. We've been friends since our first day of kindergarten. She wouldn't betray me like that." He heard the doubt in her voice, but he didn't hone in on it. He wasn't going to force her to accept something that they hadn't proven was true.

Even if it was eventually proven, he wouldn't try to convince her. She had to come to her own conclusions, make her own peace with the situation.

"You may be right, Honor. Your friend may be totally innocent of wrongdoing. I plan to speak with her as soon as I return to Boston. I'm curious to hear what she has to say," Wren said, joining the conversation.

Henry was still standing near the medical team, speaking into his cell phone. Probably filling Officer Wallace in on what had happened. Hopefully, it wouldn't take long to give statements and satisfy whatever questions the state police had.

Radley was ready to return to Boston. Being in Vermont had made him lose sight of important things—like how much he enjoyed being single, how nice it was to not be involved with a coworker, all the reasons why repeating the error he'd made with Mackenzie would be a bad idea. He needed to put some distance between himself and Honor, because she was too smart, too vibrant, too bright.

And even in the midst of terrible circumstances, she made him smile.

You really are an epic hero. If I were the kind of girl who was looking for one, you'd be exactly what I'd want to find.

But she wasn't looking for a hero, and Radley didn't want to be one. He'd been there, done that, lived to regret it.

And yet, when she'd said the words, his heart had responded as if he'd been waiting his entire life to hear them.

So he'd kissed her.

Not the kind of kiss that could ever mean anything, and somehow, it had felt like everything.

That was a problem.

A big one.

And as far as he was concerned, the only way to solve it was to go back to Boston, get back to work and forget he'd ever spent twenty-four hours trying to keep Honor alive.

TEN

Her alarm went off at 4 a.m., and Honor couldn't remember a time when she'd been so happy to hear it. She'd been lying in bed for an hour, staring up at the ceiling, listening to the old farmhouse creak and groan. The alarm was an excuse to get up and get moving. She was going to work today, and she wanted to beat rush-hour traffic. It had taken three weeks for her hands to heal enough for the doctor to clear her to return.

Three torturously long weeks.

She'd spent them on the farm with Dotty, listening to her grandmother wax poetic about Radley.

He's such a gentleman!

He's so handsome!

He knows how to saddle a horse, fix a tractor, plow a field. He loves his folks, too. Did you hear the way he talked about his mother?

As far as Dotty was concerned, Radley

could probably design a machine capable of orbiting the sun *and* diving to the bottom of the deepest ocean crevice. In one day. With six hours to spare. He was just that good.

It was tiring and tiresome.

Especially because Honor knew Radley had only visited the farm reluctantly. Absalom Winslow, AKA Kenneth Allen, had succumbed to his injuries, but the Bureau had opened a case against three of his coconspirators: Dr. Silas Proctor, Edmond Standish and Dr. Ruth McMurry. A resident of The Sanctuary had admitted to hearing them conspiring to drug Honor. Another resident claimed that Dr. McMurry had sedated Honor because she was too high-strung and needed to relax in order to truly align herself with the will of the universe. At least two witnesses had seen Edmond Standish carry Honor from her cabin. That was enough for the three to be brought in for questioning. All had lawyered up and were refusing to cooperate with the investigation. The judge might have been convinced to release them on bail if the Vermont State Police hadn't discovered a cache of cocaine hidden behind a faux wall in the meeting hall. Narcotics dogs had found traces of the drug in shipping crates used to transport clay pots to art dealers around the globe.

Apparently, The Sanctuary had been a front for a drug trafficking organization that had laundered money through the resort. Most of the residents had been unaware of the scheme. A few had suspected the truth, but none had been arrested.

The FBI had bigger fish to fry.

Radley had been assigned the case, and he was working closely with other agents to try to bring it to a close. So far, he'd found no connection between Absalom and Honor. He'd talked her through the time at The Sanctuary, probing for detail, challenging her to recall conversations and gut feelings. He'd been to the farm several times because Wren preferred interviews be conducted face-to-face rather than over the phone, and the doctor had ordered Honor to stay home.

Several times?

More like eight times.

Honor knew, because she'd counted.

Worse, she had looked forward to Radley's visits. He was a breath of fresh air after days listening to Dotty's paranoid ramblings. Since Honor's return, Dotty had worried about the farm being sold out from under her, about being forced to move into a retirement home, about losing the place where she'd spent fifty years of her life. No matter how often Honor assured her that none of those things were going to happen, no matter how many times she promised, Dotty remained obsessed with the thought.

It had gotten so bad that Honor had taken her to the doctor and asked for an evaluation. To her surprise, Dotty had passed the memory portion of the exam with flying colors.

Apparently, she wasn't suffering from dementia.

She was just plain ornery.

"What did you expect?" Bennett had asked when she'd told him about the medical exam. *"Mom has always been cussed. She'll probably outlive both of us, but she still shouldn't be on the farm by herself. She can't maintain it, and neither of us have the time to help her."*

He had said it as if Honor hadn't been spending every weekend of the past few years doing just that.

And now she'd spent three weeks of recovery doing the same. Mucking the stalls. Feeding the hens. Mowing the lawn. She'd fixed the leg on the kitchen table and applied beeswax to the old hutch. Her hands had healed more slowly because she'd done chores when she should have been resting.

She didn't mind. Not really.

She enjoyed the quiet nights and the peaceful mornings. She loved collecting eggs and watching as Dotty scrambled or fried them. But she needed to get back to work, back to having her mind humming with things other than farm life and Radley.

And Mary Alice.

Honor had reached out to her friend every day for a week, and then she'd stopped trying. According to Radley, Mary Alice continued to insist she'd had nothing to do with Absalom's plot. There'd been no phone records linking them the day of the attempted murder, nothing that indicated she was lying.

There was also no proof that she was telling the truth.

Until Honor could trust that she was, it was better to keep her distance. The loss of the friendship was a physical pain, a throbbing ache in her stomach that only seemed to dissipate when Radley was around. He really was a good distraction, asking questions and taking notes and then helping with chores that Dotty not-so-subtly mentioned.

You really are an epic hero. If I were the kind of girl who was looking for one, you'd be exactly what I'd want to find.

She'd said that to him on the rooftop.

She'd meant it.

And she really wished she could take it back.

Every time she looked him in the eye, those words were between them. Every time his arm brushed hers, or their hands accidently touched, or he leaned in close, she was reminded of his gentle kiss. They'd both been caught up in the moment, and she'd wanted to tell him that; just throw everything on the table and demand they both look at it. She didn't know how else they'd ever move on.

How *she*'d ever move on.

Radley seemed to be doing just fine.

She frowned, climbing out of bed and grabbing a suit from the closet. She tried to be quiet as she showered, dressed and pulled her hair into a high ponytail. She didn't bother with a blow-dryer. She didn't have the time or the energy to waste. If she got on the road too late, she'd be stuck in traffic for hours.

She hurried into the kitchen, grabbed a banana and an apple from the counter and tossed them into a lunch sack. She hadn't been hungry lately, but her clothes were loose, and she didn't have time to shop for new ones. Eating was a more practical solution to the problem.

She dropped the sack into her backpack. It had been returned by the Vermont police. They'd also returned her car keys, her Ford Explorer, her laptop and her phone. Everything she'd brought to The Sanctuary was back in her possession. She hadn't transported a gun to Vermont. She'd left her service weapon locked in the safe at her apartment. She'd retrieve it on her way to the office. For a moment, the thought of entering her apartment building and walking up the two flights to her floor filled her with anxiety and dread. There'd been no threats against her since she'd returned, no reason to believe she was still in danger. Absalom had called her the living sacrifice. With the amount of drugs he'd had in his system when he died, it was likely that he'd been suffering from drug-induced psychosis and that Honor had been the object of his deranged fantasy.

That was what Wren had indicated, and Honor had no reason not to believe her.

There were still days when she didn't feel safe, though. Times when a floor would creak, or fabric would rustle, and she'd be certain Absalom had survived and was waiting in the shadows to finish what he'd started.

She shuddered. Wren had sent Jessica Anderson, a criminal profiler and victims' rights advocate, to speak with Honor. Two days later, the team psychologist had paid her a visit. She'd told them that she was fine. She had meetings with both this morning. They'd make the final decision regarding whether she was ready to return to work full-time. Even with the medical doctor's okay, there were a few roadblocks that needed to be removed. The earlier she got to the office, the more relaxed she'd feel when she met with Jessica at seven.

She slid into low heels, grabbed her purse and stepped outside.

It was still dark, the sky sprinkled with stars. She'd parked the Explorer around the side of the house. She unlocked it remotely as she rounded the corner. She might not still be in danger, but the silence reminded her of the peaceful sanctuary that had once hidden a monster.

Her phone rang as she climbed into the SUV. She answered quickly, expecting the call to be work-related. She'd been away from the office for five weeks, and the backlog of cases was piling up.

"Hello?" she said, starting the engine and turning up the heat.

"Honor? It's Mary Alice. I'm sorry for calling so early, but I spoke with Special Agent Santino yesterday. She said you'd be returning to work today."

"That's right," Honor agreed, her pulse racing. She'd been hoping for this and dreading it. Their friendship had been like a cozy comforter—familiar and warm. Now it was an ill-fitting wool suit—scratchy and uncomfortable.

"I...was wondering if you'd be willing to meet with me there? I've been asked to come in for another interview, and I have an appointment with Agent Tumberg at nine."

"I can meet you before or after that," Honor said, keeping her tone even and emotionless. There was too much between them to go back to the easy repartee they'd once shared, but she wasn't going to refuse the meeting. She wanted the truth. Whatever it was. Once she had that, she could decide what to do about the friendship.

"Before would be best. I have a doctor's appointment at ten."

"Is everything okay?" Honor asked, just like she would have before the canceled wedding and the blown-off phone calls, the ignored texts and emails and the months of near silence. It was hard not to care after caring for so long, and dozens of questions popped into her mind.

"That's one of the things I want to talk to you about. I know I haven't been a good friend these past few months."

"No. You haven't."

Mary Alice was silent for a heartbeat too long, and then she sighed. "You always have been the straight shooter, Honor. Maye if I were more like you none of this would have happened."

"None of what?"

"It's…just a really hard thing to talk about."

"When I was in Vermont, you said you wanted to talk. It's been three weeks, and this is the first I've heard from you. We've been friends for years, and I love you, but I'm not going to keep chasing after the dangling carrot."

"You're angry, and I don't blame you. I'd be mad, too. I wanted to come out to the farm, but it was too awkward, and I thought it would be better to wait until you were back at work."

"Awkward? You've been at the farm hundreds of times."

"I know. I just… I'll explain everything when I see you."

"I'll be in my office by six-thirty, but I have two meetings scheduled between seven and eight. You can come to my office any time after that," Honor said.

"Right. Okay. I'll see you later." Mary Alice disconnected, and Honor sat in the Explorer, the engine rumbling, heat streaming out of the vents. She wanted to believe that Mary Alice would walk into her office, sit across from her and say a bunch of words that would make everything better. She wanted to believe that they'd both pour their hearts out the way they had when they were teens and bickering over stupid things like boys or grades or makeup choices.

They'd lived a lifetime of experience since then. College, relationships, jobs, heartaches. They'd matured, they'd learned, they'd become better able to handle whatever came their way. They shouldn't have had a spat that had kept them apart for this long, and as much as she wanted to, she couldn't believe that a meeting was going to fix whatever had broken between them.

"But You can, Lord," she whispered, and all she could do was pray that He would.

She turned on the radio, letting upbeat praise music fill the silence. She had a long day ahead, and she wanted to be focused and effective, not distracted by something that she had no control over.

She pulled around the side of the house, humming along with the music, trying to put herself in a good frame of mind, because that was what people at work would expect—upbeat, cheerful Honor. The team member most likely to be smiling. Henry had called her that once. Hopefully, she wouldn't disappoint everyone. Currently, she felt as much like smiling as she did facing rush-hour traffic.

She was halfway up the quarter-mile driveway when the engine sputtered and coughed.

Surprised, she glanced at the dashboard, realized the low-fuel light was on. It made sense. She'd driven to Vermont without fueling up. She doubted the officer who'd driven the vehicle back to her place would have thought to fill the tank. The engine sputtered again, and she coasted to the side of the drive, parking in the long grass.

She had gasoline in the barn, and she'd filled the five-gallon can before she'd left for Vermont.

She climbed out of the Explorer and headed back.

The barn was behind the house, and she walked there quickly, the cold air seeping through her suit. She had a key to the barn's side door and she unlocked it, stepping into the scent of hay and horse feed. Mice scurried in the eaves, and the barn cat darted by. She kept the gas can near the tractor, and she found it without turning on a light. She had it in her hand when someone lunged from behind a bin of feed. She whirled to defend herself, heard something whooshing through the air, felt the painful impact of something slamming into her head.

She fell, but she went fighting, clawing at a hand that pressed against her throat. Something smashed against her face, covering her mouth and nose. She inhaled without meaning to, and her mind went fuzzy, her body limp. She couldn't see a face. Just darkness and gleaming eyes. A ski mask. Light-colored eyes. The world went black, and when she came to, she was outside. Black sky. Glittering stars. Wilbur squealing and slamming against the gate to his pen. Hard earth beneath her, and someone beside her, tossing planks of wood onto the ground near her shoulder. She rolled onto her side, trying to get to her knees, but he was there again. Ski mask and chemical-soaked cloth, cursing under his breath, and she felt the way she had in the hospital—as if she should know something but didn't.

Wilbur was still squealing, and she could see him trotting in her direction, his two-hundred-pound body gleaming in the predawn gray. And then she was being dragged across the grass, pushed over what felt like a rocky ledge. It took her too long to realize what it was, where she was. The old well. The one that had been boarded up years ago. It wasn't boarded now, and she was being shoved over the edge. She tried to stop her fall, grabbing for the stone wall. It crumbled, and she barely managed to find another handhold.

Wilbur's yelps grew louder, and the man howled, cursing again. Wilbur must have bitten him. Hopefully, he'd repeat the offense. She had her toes wedged in cracks in the interior wall of the well. She levered up, her hands still holding onto the ledge. She managed to get her shoulders up and out, but the man was there again, rag pressed to her face, shoving her backward, and this time she couldn't grab the wall. She tumbled into the darkness, hands and feet scrabbling against old stone and slick moss as she fell.

Radley had spent countless hours poring over Honor's case. He'd combed through evidence, conducted interviews, attempted to find a reason why Absalom Winslow had wanted Honor dead. Wren seemed to think the attempted murder had been the product of drug-induced paranoia. She'd presented that idea to the team at their last meeting. He couldn't deny that it had merit. The fact was, all the evidence seemed to point in that direction. Aside from Mary Alice, there was no connection between Honor and Absalom. Mary Alice had submitted to and passed a polygraph, she'd allowed herself to be interviewed twice, and she'd agreed to come in again. From what Radley could ascertain, she was being honest when she said she hadn't hired Absalom to harm

Honor, hadn't plotted with him to do that and hadn't helped him in his efforts.

What would she have gained from doing any of those things? He'd seen her bank records when he'd checked to make sure she hadn't withdrawn or deposited large amounts of money recently. She was, as Honor had indicated, wealthy. She seemed to be financially responsible. No large debts. No properties going into foreclosure or overdrawn bank accounts. She'd taken a leave of absence from her job five months after she'd called off her wedding, but she had enough money to not have to work for the rest of her life.

If Mary Alice was involved, it wasn't for financial gain.

And he couldn't think of any other motive she might have. Neither woman had a significant other, so there shouldn't be jealousy issues. He'd spoken to mutual friends. He'd interviewed Mary Alice's parents. He'd spoken with her friends. As far as they were all concerned, Mary Alice had gone to a spiritual sanctuary to try to put her life back together after a devastating breakup.

He tapped a pencil on his desk, staring at the mug shot that was lying on top of several other papers. Absalom had been younger in it, his face not as gaunt, his eyes not as shadowed or empty-looking. He'd still been going by the name Kenneth Allen, but he'd already had a two-page rap sheet. Petty stuff mostly. Possession. DUI. Simple assault. His mother had made the call once, accusing him of battery when he was eighteen. She had a rap sheet, too, and was doing time for ID theft and extortion. She'd taken photos of the manager of the building she cleaned and threatened to go to his wife with proof that he was having an affair.

Based on phone records and email accounts, it didn't look like Absalom had had contact with his mother in the past few years. She'd been informed of her son's death, and Radley planned to meet with her at the end of the week to discuss her son. He doubted she'd have anything helpful to say, but he had to follow the lead and see where it led.

Someone tapped on his door.

"Come in," he called, gathering the papers and stacking them neatly in a file folder.

The door opened and Jessica Anderson entered. Five-foot-nothing with light brown skin and vivid green eyes, she'd been recruited from her job with the state police and had joined the unit a month ago.

"Agent Tumberg, I hope I'm not interrupting

anything important," she said, her tone formal and a little stiff.

"Not at all. Would you like to have a seat?"

"No. Thank you." She smiled, but it didn't reach her eyes. "It's early, and I haven't had coffee, so I'll cut to the chase. I was supposed to meet Agent Remington in her office twenty minutes ago. Agent Santino asked me to make sure her transition back to work goes smoothly."

"Honor *has* been through a lot," he agreed, even though she hadn't asked his opinion. He'd been trying to stay as emotionally removed from the case as he could. It had been a lot more difficult than he'd have liked.

Honor was a coworker, and that would have made it hard enough. But the time they'd spent in Vermont had forged a bond between them. No matter how much he tried to deny it, no matter how many times he told himself nothing had changed between them, the facts were the same—he couldn't look at Honor without seeing a woman he admired and liked and enjoyed spending time with. He couldn't listen to her voice and not think about those moments on the rooftop, her sweet, silly words, her act of heroism, the way her lips had felt beneath his.

"She hasn't arrived," Jessica stated bluntly, the words like ice water through his veins.

"You're sure?" He could think of a few things that might have kept her from work. Dotty. Traffic. A medical emergency. He couldn't think of any that would have kept her from calling to reschedule meetings she was going to be late for.

"Yes. I called her cell and home phone. No answer on either. I've got to admit, I'm worried."

He grabbed the desk phone, dialing Honor's number quickly. It went directly to voice mail. He left a terse message for her to call and then tried her home number. This time, he heard the distinctive click of someone lifting the receiver.

"Hello? Who is this? Why are you calling me this time of day? Don't you know that decent people are in bed this time of day?" a woman demanded.

"Ms. Dotty?" he guessed, and she huffed.

"Who wants to know?"

"Radley Tumberg. Honor's coworker."

"Radley! How are you, dear? When do you plan to visit again? We have a drippy faucet in the bathroom that could really use a man's touch."

"I can stop by this weekend."

"Wonderful! I'll make you a nice meal. Honor will help. She's a great cook. Have I mentioned that?"

"A few times." Just like she'd mentioned that Honor knew how to change a tractor tire, sew on a button, saddle a horse and plow a field. Every time he was at the farm, he got a dozen hints that he and Honor might be a perfect match. "Speaking of Honor, has she left for work yet?"

"She planned to leave before five. You know how she is. Always worried about punctuality."

"Did she leave on schedule?" he persisted, because Dotty hadn't answered the question, and he needed to know.

"I'm sure she did. Honor always does what she says she will, but I can check her room if you'd like me to."

"I would. Thanks." He met Jessica's eyes. He could see his concern reflected there.

"Is everything okay, Radley?" Dotty asked. "You sound upset."

"I just...wanted to make sure Honor was on the way in."

"She should be there. Her door is open. She's not in the room. Not in the bathroom. I'm looking out the window, and her car is gone."

"All right. Thank you. I'll see you this weekend," he said, not wanting her to know how worried he was.

"Young man," she barked before he could hang up. "I may be old, but I'm not stupid. Tell me what's wrong."

"We don't know that anything is," he hedged, but he felt the truth in his gut.

"Is she there?"

"Not yet."

"Then something *is* wrong. I'm calling my son. He'll bring me out your way. We'll look for the car. Maybe she had a flat tire."

She hung up, and he placed the phone in the receiver. Met Jessica's eyes. "I don't like this."

"Do you want me to call Agent Santino?"

"Yes. I'll call the county and state police. Ask them to put out an APB on her car."

His cell phone rang, and he pulled it out, hoping it was Honor explaining why she was running late.

Instead, he saw Dotty's home number. His heart leaped. Maybe she'd made a mistake. Maybe Honor was still in the house. "Hello?"

"I found her car," Dotty announced without preamble.

"So she is still home?" He dropped into the chair, his legs almost weak with relief. He didn't allow himself to dwell on what that meant.

"I don't think so. I was getting ready to call

Bennett, and I looked out my bedroom window. I can see the driveway from there, and I am pretty certain I can see her car parked off to the side of it. I'm going to walk out there and take a look, but I thought I'd call you first."

"No!" he nearly shouted, and then he schooled his voice and his tone and tried again. "What I mean is that it's probably best if you call the local police and have them check it out."

"Because you think something happened to her. Something you don't want me to see," she said.

"I don't know what's going on, but if someone is out there, someone dangerous, I don't want you out there, too."

"I appreciate your concern, but I have my husband's shotgun, and I'll take it with me."

"Ms. Dotty," he began, but he heard the quiet click as she disconnected, and he knew she was heading off to do exactly what she'd said.

He grabbed his suit jacket from the back of his chair, shrugging it on as he ran into the hall. He couldn't shake the image of Honor's SUV abandoned beside her driveway. He couldn't stop mentally listing all the reasons why she might have stopped there.

None of them were good.

He'd seen her two days ago, and they'd discussed the case. He'd assured her, just as he knew Wren had been doing, that the agency believed the threat against her had been neutralized when Absalom died. He'd had no guarantee of that, no proof, and he'd known it when he'd spoken the words. He'd been honest. He'd given her the facts they'd gathered, but he hadn't told her to be careful, he hadn't reminded her that they weren't sure of anything yet.

He hadn't said that he worried about her. That he enjoyed spending time with her. That he missed her when they weren't together.

He hadn't wanted to break the vow he'd made to himself. He hadn't wanted to repeat the mistake he'd made with Mackenzie. Neither of those reasons seemed important now.

The only thing that mattered, the only thing he cared about, was finding Honor and making sure she was okay.

ELEVEN

She dreamed of icebergs and snowmen, of building forts out of old fence posts and making snowballs with ungloved hands. In her dreams, she was cold, her body stiff, her feet numb.

Move! her dream-self kept demanding. *Move or die.*

And she tried, but her body didn't work, and she realized she was covered in snow, frozen in place. In this dream everything was blue and white ice and shaking agony, the blanket of snow building and building, covering her chin and her cheeks and then her mouth and nose.

She inhaled, sputtering and gasping, coughing and gagging, the snow replaced by water.

And she realized she was no longer dreaming.

She was awake, lying in a dark space filled with water and cold.

Not a dark space.

A well.

The well. The one she'd been tossed into.

Fifteen feet deep. Four feet in diameter. Not a good place to die, but she knew it was intended to be her tomb.

For a moment, she was so panicked she couldn't think. She could only act, jumping up, clawing at the walls, screaming and screaming and screaming. Breaking nails, scraping palms, trying to muscle her way from the bottom of the well to the top of it. Yelling until her throat was raw, her voice hoarse, her head pounding with the effort.

Or from the bump she'd received when she'd fallen.

She could feel it throbbing at the back of her head, and she touched the area, probing the bump. No blood. No broken skin. She didn't feel dizzy, light-headed or disoriented, so she'd work under the assumption that she didn't have a concussion or a brain bleed; that her biggest, most pressing problem was that she was trapped in a well with just about no hope of escaping it.

"No hope? You're alive. You didn't break your neck or your skull, so stop panicking and think," she muttered, the words echoing hoarsely.

She had no idea how long she'd been there,

but she could see the sun gleaming above the well. It was at its zenith, a bright yellow orb against the robin's-egg-blue sky, endlessly far away. Absolutely unreachable.

But the crumbling edge of the old well was not.

She refused to allow it to be, because she refused to die on her grandmother's property, a few hundred feet away from safety.

She shivered, sloshing through knee-deep water, her clothes soaked, her teeth chattering. She wasn't going to give whoever had tossed her the satisfaction of knowing he'd succeeded. She wasn't going to let him have the final words in the story of her life.

She was finding a way out, she was going to figure out who'd shoved her in and she was going to make him pay.

She just hoped God agreed with her plan, but she'd need a miracle to achieve her goal, superhuman strength that would let her scale the wall like Spider-Man, fly out of it like some avenging wraith.

Of course, she didn't expect to be zapped with either of those abilities, but divine inspiration would be nice; some finite and feasible plan that would get her out.

"Come on, Honor," she muttered. "Think. There has to be a way."

The words echoed hollowly, mixing with the splash of her legs through the water. She touched the wall, sliding her hands along the cool stone. It was slick with algae, rough with lichen. If Radley were there, he'd probably have some handy tool tucked in a pocket that he could use to crawl out. She didn't have anything. She'd left her purse in the SUV, her cell phone with it. Even if someone found the Explorer, it would take time to find her.

The sun would probably set before then.

Hopefully not for the last time in her life.

She wasn't afraid to die, but she'd like to live a while longer.

She surveyed the interior of the well again, looking for anything that could help in her effort to escape. She slid her feet through the murky water, but there were no old boards or planks lying beneath the surface. She'd checked again and again, and then once more, because she refused to believe there was nothing. No boards. No rope. No whistle or siren or alarm. No handy ladder that would lead her up and out. Hope was like that—unreasonably certain of a good outcome. Even in the face of evidence against it.

"Of course, you're going to have a good outcome. You have meetings today. At some point, someone at work will realize you're not there. People will be dispatched to find you. They'll search the property, discover the well and pull you out," she told herself.

It made sense. It was a reasonable expectation, but she'd been in the well since before dawn, and if the position of the sun in the sky were any indication, it was after noon.

People at work should have already arrived.

The police should have been here long ago.

She should be out of her tomb, free from her grave, sitting at her desk trying to figure out why the voice of her attacker had sounded so familiar. It had to have been one of Absalom's guards. Or maybe someone she'd met at the compound. She couldn't put the voice to a face or a name, but she would. She had to. She wanted this over. All the danger, the fear, the worry. She wanted to go back to the office—just like she'd planned—and get back to work solving other people's problems, because she was tired of living in the midst of her own.

Because it was hard. Not just being attacked, thrown in a well, targeted for death. That stuff was difficult, scary and daunting. It was the not knowing, though, that was eating at her. Not knowing why. Not knowing who. Not knowing whom she could trust and whom she couldn't.

Not knowing where the next moment would lead, because she had no idea what was motivating the attacks or how to stop them. She wanted her life back.

In all its boring routine and simplicity—the long days at the office, the nights in her apartment, the weekends on the farm. She wanted church on Sunday and prayers in the wee hours of the mornings. Long hikes and lazy evenings, and Radley sitting by her side.

The thought brought her up short, and she tried to push it away. This wasn't the time to think about Radley or to worry about what their relationship might be. Could be.

What she wanted it to be.

This was the time for coming up with a plan. She couldn't stay in the well overnight. She was already shaking with cold.

Please, God, she prayed silently. *Help me find a way out of this.*

She'd seen online videos of young kids scaling walls by pressing their backs against one side and their feet against the other. It had looked easy enough. Of course, they'd been in hallways that were narrower than the mouth of the well. She had to try anyway, because she wasn't going to stand around waiting for rescue.

She leaned her shoulders against one wall,

put a foot on the wall across from it and inched upward. It wasn't easy. It wasn't quick, but she was doing it. Slowly creeping upward. Her feet slipped in thick algae, and she couldn't catch herself. She fell with a splash, scrambled upright.

She could hear Wilbur squealing. He had to have escaped his pen. Usually, he'd wander over to the neighbors. But this time, he seemed to be hanging out close to the well.

"Wilbur, go get help!" she shouted as if he were a beautifully groomed collie wandering around looking for people to rescue rather than a huge lumbering pig who'd rather take a chunk out of someone than help them.

"Wilbur, I feed you, remember?" she called. "I bring you pieces of Dotty's apple pie. If I die down here, who's going to do that?"

Wilbur grunted a few more times, then went silent. Knowing him, Honor was sure he'd found some sweet grass shoots nearby and was nibbling them while she died.

"You are not going to die," she growled, facing the wall, hands on slippery rocks. She stepped back, stretching until her feet were touching the opposite wall, and then she tried to climb up again. One hand at a time, one foot at a time, perched over the water, bowed like an inchworm. If the walls hadn't been so slippery, she might have made it, but she couldn't get enough leverage, and she fell again, her head slamming into rock.

Stunned, she lay in the water, breathless, disoriented.

She thought she heard someone shouting. At first it seemed like a figment of her imagination, maybe a trick of her auditory system. The well produced strange echoes of sound, and she thought she might be hearing her breath amplified a dozen-fold.

But the sound had more substance, and she stood, straining to hear.

There it was again! Someone shouting. Maybe her name. Maybe something else. It didn't matter. They were close enough for her to hear. If she could get their attention, she'd be free.

She crouched, sliding her hands through the water, searching for the loose rocks that were lying at the bottom of the well. She found one, hefted it from the water and began slamming it against the wall, trying to mimic Morse code for SOS. Dot-dot-dot. Dash-dash-dash. Dot-dot-dot.

Over and over again.

Her fingers went numb from the force of

the blows. Her arms went numb. Her muscles strained and trembled, but she couldn't quit.

If someone was up there, she wanted to be heard.

She wanted to be rescued.

She wanted to find the person responsible for tossing her down there and make him pay, and then she wanted to go back to her job, her beautiful life, to Dotty.

And to Radley, her heart added.

She ignored it and continued pounding the code, praying that someone would hear.

It had taken too long to get to the farm. By the time Radley arrived, the local police had been on the scene for two hours. They'd combed through the evidence left at the Explorer, shouted for Honor over and over again, walking into the fields that bordered the driveway, searching for signs that she'd been there. They'd found no evidence of a struggle, no indication that Honor had been attacked near her SUV. The police had concluded that she'd run out of gas, gotten out of the vehicle and disappeared.

Only people didn't disappear.

They walked away, went into hiding, started new lives. They were abducted by strangers or friends, held captive, hidden away. They were mistreated, abused, kept in captivity or released, allowed to live or murdered.

There were dozens of possibilities when a person was missing, but no one just fell off the face of the earth and disappeared.

Honor was somewhere.

They just had to find her.

He searched the grassy areas around the Explorer, looking for anything the police might have missed. It wasn't that he didn't trust their work. He knew they'd been thorough, but he had to see for himself, he had to check every possibility.

"See anything?" Wren called as she strode up the driveway. She'd been interviewing Dotty, talking to neighbors, trying to find out if anyone had heard anything.

"Nothing."

"The local police believe she was transported off the farm. There is evidence that a vehicle was parked off the road a few yards from here."

"I know." He'd spoken to Sheriff Ethan Cartwright. The guy had a good head on his shoulders and about twenty more years of law enforcement experience than Radley. Cartwright had made his position known. He felt strongly that Honor had been taken off the farm, that she was with her attacker, heading away from the scene of the abduction. He and his deputies were focusing on the area surrounding Honor's SUV, trying to put together a clearer picture of what had occurred.

"Did you know they found blood evidence near there?"

He stopped searching the grass and met Wren's eyes. They both knew that changed things. That the situation had just gone from serious to dire. "No."

"Just a few drops in the grass."

"Any amount of blood is concerning."

"I agree. I'm calling in the department's evidence team. The sheriff has agreed to it. If we had a description of the vehicle that was parked near where the blood was found, we could issue an APB." She shook her head, looking more worried than he'd ever seen her.

"How about K-9 teams? Does the sheriff's office have them?" he asked.

"They'll be here shortly. It's a long shot, though. The sheriff said the dogs have been able to track vehicle-carried scents, but not for a very long distance. If Honor was taken by car, it's going to be difficult for them to follow her trail."

He nodded, walking back to Honor's SUV. The doors were closed. The engine was off.

She'd left it that way. She'd also left the keys in the ignition, her purse on the seat.

"What I can't wrap my head around," he murmured aloud, "is the fact that there's no evidence of a struggle here and none on the road. We've got no scuff marks on the driveway. No tamped-down areas of grass."

"We have blood down the road in an area where another vehicle was parked. Don't downplay that evidence."

"Is there a sign of a struggle near the blood?" he questioned, and she frowned.

"What are you thinking?"

"That Honor isn't the kind of person to allow herself to be taken without a fight. If someone approached her here, there'd be some sign of it."

"I agree, but as I keep mentioning, blood has been found. That's an indicator of struggle."

"No scuffed earth. No broken grass. There's nothing, Wren."

"There may be at the other scene. How about we walk over and take a look?"

"But, how did she get from here to there without putting up a fight?" he asked, still not willing to leave the scene. Something was niggling at the back of his mind, telling him that things weren't what they seemed, that Honor might not be far as they were all imagining.

He couldn't ignore that.

He wouldn't.

"Radley, I know you don't want to believe she's been kidnapped—"

"There's no doubt she's gone, but we don't know how far she's been taken. For all we know, she's somewhere nearby. The area where the other vehicle was parked is in that direction, right?" He pointed toward the road.

"Right, and she'd have passed it if she were heading toward town to get gas."

"Why would she go for gas without her purse or phone? And, why walk? Dotty has a vehicle. Why not go back to the house, grab the keys and drive herself to the nearest gas station? Or even take Dotty's car to work and get gas on the way home?"

"Good question. And, you're right. It doesn't make sense. If she were abducted here, she'd have struggled. If she were abducted up the road, she should have had her purse and phone with her."

She turned so she was facing the farmhouse. It was less than a quarter mile away. Two-story and quaint, the roofline steep, the eaves decorated with gingerbread trim. He'd spent a lot of time in the house. He'd spent time on the wraparound porch, watching the sunset as he listened to Honor and Dotty chat.

He could have spent a lifetime there, and it wouldn't have felt like enough. Not if Honor was there with him.

"It's an easy walk back to the house. If I were here, that's where I'd have headed. So, what happened between here and there? Was she approached from behind? Surprised? Carried away?"

"Or, not? What if she wasn't taken from the farm?" he asked, and Wren frowned.

"You're suggesting this was staged?"

"I'm not suggesting anything. I'm tossing out questions, hoping there will be answers that make sense."

"Answers would be good, but in lieu of them, I'd like to have a lot more manpower on the ground here." She pulled out her cell phone and sent a quick text. "I've asked Jessica and Henry to meet us here. We can fan out and do a more thorough search of the area. If she was taken somewhere on the farm, there should be some sign of that."

"Right," he agreed, as if they were talking about taking out the trash or tossing out an old piece of furniture.

But they weren't.

They were discussing Honor. Vibrant. Funny. Smart. Energetic. Beautiful.

He couldn't think of her without thinking

about those things, and he wished he'd told her that the last time he'd seen her. And the time before that and before that. He wished he'd let himself go to that place where he could admit to himself and to her that she took up space in his mind, in his life, in his heart.

But he'd wanted to protect himself, wanted to avoid trouble, wanted to play it safe. And he hadn't said what he could when he should have. He could only pray it wasn't too late.

A marked police car turned onto the driveway, rumbling toward them and parking nearby. The driver and passenger doors opened in tandem, a female sheriff's deputy and Bennett Remington emerging from the vehicle. The deputy opened a back door, and Mary Alice stepped out. Tall and thin, dressed in fitted black pants and a light purple sweater set, she had her hair pulled back into a tight bun, her face makeup-free. She'd been crying. He could see that immediately. Her eyes were red-rimmed and swollen, her lids puffy.

"Have you found her?" Bennett demanded before anyone could speak.

"Mr. Remington," Wren replied. "I know this is upsetting, but we have a lot of work to do. I can assure you, as soon as we find your niece, you'll be informed of it. The best thing you can do is go wait with your mother. She's very upset and could use some support."

"My mother knows how to handle herself, and she'll understand if I'm out here trying to get to the bottom of the situation. As for being informed… That's a laugh. I wouldn't even know she was missing if my mother hadn't called me."

"Dotty let us know you were on the way. If she hadn't, I can assure you, we would have called you to update you on the situation," Wren explained calmly. Better her than Radley. He wasn't in the mood for dealing with Bennett's faux indignation. As far as he could tell, the guy couldn't care less about his niece. He'd never visited her in the hospital, he rarely called. He might have been her guardian when she was young, but he certainly hadn't filled the role of father. He'd given her what was necessary to get her through her childhood and her teen years, and then he'd let her go her way while he went his. Dotty was the tie that bound them together.

"How could this have happened?" Mary Alice asked, her face pale, her red hair gleaming like fire in the afternoon sun. Unlike Bennett, she looked sincerely concerned and alarmed. "I just spoke to her this morning, and she was fine."

"What time was that?" Radley asked, his nerves jumping to attention, his mind grabbing at the new information.

"Maybe 4:30. I knew I was going to be at your offices, and I wanted to meet with her. We haven't had a chance to talk, and I thought it was time."

"Did she mention going into work?"

"She said she was on her way. We ended the call, and I assumed she'd be at the office when I arrived." Her voice caught and tears slid down her cheeks. "I should have told her I loved her before I hung up. We always said that to each other. Until recently." Her gaze shifted to Bennett, and there was something in her eyes that captured Radley's attention, that made him want to explore that relationship a little more deeply.

"We think someone was waiting for her to leave the house and grabbed her when her car ran out of gas," Wren explained.

"But..." Her voice trailed off, and she was still watching Bennett. He seemed oblivious, his attention on the Explorer.

"What?" Radley prodded, hoping she'd continue with whatever she'd planned to say.

"Honor never runs out of gas," Mary Alice finally said.

"Don't be absurd, Mary Alice," Bennett

nearly spat, whirling to face them again. "Of course, she does. The evidence is sitting right in front of us." He gestured at the vehicle, then stalked into the middle of the driveway. There was a slight hitch in his stride, a small limp that he hadn't had the last time Radley questioned him.

"Are you injured, Mr. Remington?" he asked, and Bennett scowled.

"Pardon?"

"It looks like you're limping."

"I twisted my ankle while I was out running. A nasty sprain, the doctor said. Not that it matters. We need to focus on finding my niece and bringing her home."

"I thought you only ran on the treadmill," Mary Alice said, and the thing Radley had seen in her eyes was now in her voice. Something dark and ugly. Not anger. Maybe disgust.

"How would you know anything about me? You're Honor's friend. Not mine."

"Right. Sure," she replied, turning away from him, scanning the area, her gaze drifting across the landscape. Lush fields. Colorful maple trees. The brilliant blue sky.

Radley could almost hear her cataloguing the details.

Finally, she shook her head. "I'm still not buying it. Honor is meticulous about safety.

She always fills her gas tank before she leaves on a trip. I know she hasn't been driving since she arrived home. Dotty refuses to drive the Explorer because it's too big a vehicle. So, why was there no gas in the tank?"

"Honor wasn't the last person to drive the vehicle," Wren pointed out gently. She understood, as Radley did, that loved ones often refused to believe that people they cared about were victims of crimes. "The Vermont State Police transported it here for her."

"It's not that far a drive to Vermont. Two hours. Maybe a little more. Like I said, Honor would have filled up the gas tank before she left home. I find it really difficult to believe the tank was empty when the police brought it back here," Mary Alice insisted. For the first time since Radley had met her, she looked confident and self-assured. Strong. It was as if she had found something to fight for, and she was going to do it with everything she had. "Even if she did run out of gas, there's always a five-gallon jug of it in the barn with the tractor. All she'd have had to do was bring it out here and fill the tank."

And that was it.

The missing piece to the puzzle.

He met Wren's eye.

"The barn," he said. "Whoever it was knew

she kept a can of gasoline there. He siphoned the fuel from the tank and waited for her in the barn. She wouldn't have been expecting an attack. She'd have walked in blind and unprepared and been ambushed."

"Inform the sheriff. He'll need to bring his evidence team," Wren called to the deputy who was already on her radio.

Radley sprinted across the grassy field that separated the driveway from a sea of yellow cornstalks. Beyond that, the barn was brick red against the stunning blue sky. No clouds. No thunder. No hint that the day had gone from good to horrible, but the barn was just ahead, the doors yawning open. He'd been to the farm enough to know that Honor never left them that way.

He sprinted across the threshold, skidding to a stop a few steps in. The tractor was there. The gas can—tipped on its side. A rag lay beside it. There were scuff marks in the dirt floor, obvious evidence of a struggle. And he knew Honor had fought, that she'd made every attempt to escape.

He stepped closer, ignoring Wren's warning to be careful, to be sure he didn't contaminate the scene. He could clearly see two sets of footprints in the dirt. He could see the disturbed earth where Honor had fought. No blood, and that gave him hope. He didn't want to believe she'd been critically injured.

He wouldn't believe it.

Jessica and Henry entered the barn. He didn't have to explain. They both knew what they were seeing.

"What do you think?" Jessica asked, crouching near the door and studying the floor from her position there.

"He ambushed her. They fought," he responded, eyeing the scuff marks, trying to put aside his emotions and think like the law enforcement officer he was. "He dragged her backward, and then he carried her." He pointed to a set of footprints moving away from the scene.

"Carried her where?" Jessica asked. "The door is over here. Those footprints are moving in the opposite direction."

"There's another door. It goes out to the horse pasture and pig pen."

"On a farm like this, there are plenty of places to hide someone," Henry added. "He wouldn't have had to take her to a vehicle. He could have dropped her somewhere and left her. Maybe he planned to return later."

Or, maybe, he hadn't thought he'd need to.

None of them said it, but Radley knew they

were thinking it. In their line of work, they saw the worst of humanity.

He moved through the barn without speaking. The door into the pasture was open, and he walked through, following the prints into the grassy field that the horses grazed on.

A few yards out, something lay in the grass, a crumbled mass nearly hidden by knee-high grass.

"Honor," he shouted, running toward it.

Suddenly, the mass lunged up, and he realized he wasn't looking at a fallen woman. He was looking at a huge pig.

Wilbur squealed angrily, but instead of charging toward Radley, he lumbered away. Screeching loudly, scuffling at the dirt at the edge of the fenced area.

He huffed again, took a few steps toward Radley, and then went back to what he was doing. Grunting and digging as if there were something buried…

Radley's heart stopped.

He felt it freeze in his chest, his entire body going cold as he raced through the grass and braced himself for what he might find.

He saw the old well before he reached it—gray rock edging up four feet from the ground, several planks lying nearby.

And he knew.

He knew she was there. That she'd been carried from the barn and dropped into the well.

"Honor!" he shouted again, and the soft tap of rock hitting rock answered.

Three short. Three long. Three short.

SOS.

He reached the edge of the well, Wren right beside him a Maglite in hand. She aimed it down into the well, and Honor was there. Staring up at them. Face smeared with dirt, eyes glowing hotly in her pale face. Water up to her knees, clothes clinging to her skin.

"I was wondering how long it would take you to find me," she said, smiling broadly.

And that smile?

It settled in his heart like the best gift he'd ever received, like the most precious treasure he'd ever found.

"So," she continued, as she dropped the rock, let it splash into the water. "Now that you've all finally arrived, how about you get me out of here?"

TWELVE

Honor hadn't realized how much she enjoyed her freedom until she didn't have it anymore. Three days had passed since she'd been pushed into the well, and they still had no idea who'd done it. As a precaution, Wren had insisted Honor have twenty-four-hour protection. They'd considered moving her to a safe house, but she'd refused. She hadn't wanted to leave Dotty again, and Dotty had been dead set against leaving the farmhouse.

Currently, Radley and Jessica were staying at the farm. They escorted Honor to work and back. They stayed overnight in the guest rooms. In three days, they'd woven their way into the fabric of the farm's life.

Dotty was ecstatic, the extra people reminding her of how life had been when her husband was alive and her sons were still at home. She'd told Honor that while they'd made apple pie and homemade ice cream the previous evening. Honor wanted to be happy for her grandmother. The situation was bringing her no end of joy. But she worried about the disappointment and heartache Dotty would feel when this was over and Radley and Jessica went back to their lives.

The house would be empty again.

The days long and lonely.

Maybe Uncle Bennett had been right when he'd suggested that Dotty would be better off in a retirement home. That had been seven or eight months ago. Honor had been busy helping Mary Alice prepare for her wedding, and she'd been too distracted to listen to the detailed description he gave of the wonderful retirement villages. She remembered him talking about community, friendship, games, companionship.

She also remembered how livid Dotty had been when he'd broached the subject with her. She had no intention of moving anywhere. The farm was where she'd spent the last fifty-three years of her life, and it was where she planned to stay until the day she died.

She'd made the pronouncement then, and she'd continued to make it every few days since.

Honor sighed, glancing at the clock on the bedside table. It was two in the morning, and she was wide awake, trapped in her room because Radley and Jessica were sleeping a few doors away.

Who was she kidding?

She didn't care if Jessica heard her wandering around.

It was Radley she was trying to avoid.

Avoid?

That was an exaggeration.

She wasn't avoiding him. She was avoiding the conversation she knew they needed to have. The one about the way she'd felt when she'd looked up and seen him at the top of the well. There'd been three other people with him, and his was the only face she remembered. His were the arms she'd walked into when they'd finally managed to toss down a rope and help her rappel up. It had felt so right to be there that she'd forgotten her coworkers, the police, Dotty and Mary Alice. She'd completely tuned out her uncle's disapproving glare. His arms had been home, and she hadn't wanted to leave.

But life happened, and time ticked by one moment at a time.

The world didn't stop because a woman had fallen head over heels for a guy she worked with. There'd been no time to discuss anything but the case, no opportunity to ask Radley if what she felt when she looked into his eyes was reciprocated.

She sighed. If she and Mary Alice were still close, she'd have discussed the situation with her. As it was, because of the timing of her early morning phone call, the police and FBI suspected that Mary Alice had been working with Honor's attacker.

Honor understood their reasoning. She could see the case from their points of view, but she still didn't want to believe that her best friend would betray her like that.

She'd wanted to go to the precinct and be there when the police interviewed Mary Alice, but Wren had thought it was too dangerous. She'd asked that there be no contact between Honor and her best friend, and that had been hard. Cutting ties, refusing phone calls, allowing herself to pull away from the one friend she'd had since childhood.

She loved Mary Alice like a sister.

She wanted to trust her.

But she didn't.

Not really.

And that hurt almost as much as knowing her friend was still keeping secrets.

Frustrated, unable to stand one more minute of pacing her room, Honor eased open the door and stepped into the hall. Up until the last month, she'd thought she had life figured out. Sure, she'd been worried about Dotty and Mary Alice, but she hadn't thought any of their problems were insurmountable. She'd believed, hoped and trusted that things would work out. She'd expected life to go on just the way it had been—smooth sailing with just a few daunting waves along the way.

And then she'd gone to The Sanctuary. She'd nearly been killed. She'd realized that the problems she was facing were way more complicated than she'd thought.

God was still good.

Dotty loved to say that. Honor remembered the words being murmured in her ear the day of her parents' funeral. Tears had been streaming down Dotty's face, but she'd hugged Honor tight and told her that.

Honor had believed it then.

As she'd matured and grown, she'd learned to believe it in a deeper way, to understand that God's goodness was not measured by life circumstance.

Circumstances changed.

God did not.

"And He is still good," she whispered as she walked downstairs and into the kitchen.

"Always," Radley responded.

She leaped a foot, whirling to face him.

"You're quiet as a cat," she said. "You need to do something about that."

"Like?"

"Wear a bell around your neck?" she suggested, and he laughed, the sound warm and full. No holding back with Radley. He was what he appeared to be. All about justice and his job and protecting people he cared about.

"That might be difficult to explain around the office."

"You never know. Our coworkers might appreciate it." She grabbed the kettle and filled it, lighting the gas burner before she turned to face him.

"You look tired," he commented.

"Funny, I was just thinking you look great," she responded. He did—dark jeans, blue flannel shirt, hair just a little mussed.

"Just so you know, the fact that you look tired doesn't mean you don't also look great. You're a beautiful woman, Honor. Even dressed in pig-print pajamas."

She glanced down, realized she was wearing the joke-gift Mary Alice had given her two Christmases ago. "These were from Mary Alice. She'd told me Wilbur was going to be a big pig. I told her that he'd be the size of a small cat. When he reached a hundred pounds, she took his photo and had these made."

"You smile when you tell the story," he said.

"It's a good memory."

"And a good thing Mary Alice was right. We think Wilbur is the reason your attacker didn't kill you before he threw you in the well. We found blood on the boards that were covering the well, a few drops on the grass and some on the dirt near the barn. We also found them on Wilbur's muzzle."

"Are you telling me," she asked, trying not to smile when she thought about it. "That you swabbed the pig's snout to see if he bit my attacker?"

"It was Wren's idea. She noticed he had some discoloration on his face."

"So, Wilbur is a guard pig," she murmured, smiling full-out, because the little pot-belly pig she'd laughed at Dotty for getting had come more in handy than she ever would have imagined he could.

"That about sums it up."

"Wow. Just...wow. That's amazing."

"The fact that he tried to protect you? Or that we swabbed him for blood?"

"The fact that a tiny little potbelly pig could grow into a vicious attack animal. God is certainly creative when it comes to saving the hides of His children," she said with a laugh.

"He is that," he replied, smiling as he watched

her. And, her laughter died, her smile faded away, because he was there, and they were alone, and being with him still felt right.

"You need to stop worrying," he murmured, tucking a strand of hair behind her ears.

"Who says I'm worrying?"

"The frown line between your brows."

"I don't have one," she retorted, but she touched the area anyway. "Do I?"

"Only when you frown."

"I don't frown. Much."

"I know this is a tough time, Honor, but don't give up hope that Mary Alice's name will be cleared," he said, as if he'd been sitting inside her head, listening to the worries that had kept her awake.

"I'm not giving up hope, but as an investigator, I'd be a fool not to realize how guilty she looks."

"She's the perfect scapegoat."

"What do you mean?"

"She has means to betray you. Maybe not motive, but she's certainly not proving to anyone that she doesn't want you dead."

She winced.

"Sorry. That was blunt."

"It's okay. Go ahead with your train of thought. I'm curious to see where you're heading."

"Aside from means and knowledge, she

has no alibi and no explanation for how she connected with Absalom. She sidesteps more questions than she answers. She's vague about her reasons for going to The Sanctuary. She refuses to reveal who told her about it. Overall, it's not looking good."

"We've established all that, Radley," she said wearily. She felt weary. Of the questions, the lack of answers, the feeling that she couldn't trust her closest friend.

"We have, but we haven't established why an intelligent woman, one who has to know that she's in trouble, wouldn't at least try to give us explanations. She hasn't made up a story, hasn't tossed us any leads. Why just continue to refuse to answer?"

"Mary Alice has high ethical and moral values. She tries to be honest whenever she can."

"And when she can't?"

"She stays silent."

"Then, maybe we should be looking at this from a different angle."

"What do you mean?"

"She won't give us information that will clear her name. There must be a reason. Someone she's protecting or something she's hiding because she's afraid. What does she care about, Honor?"

"Up until a few months ago, I would have said her family and me. Her job."

"She took a leave of absence from that."

"Right. To get her head together after Scott cheated."

"So we're down to you and her family."

"Like I said, a few months ago, I would have thought she cared most about those things. Now, I don't know."

"Maybe it's time to find out."

"What do you mean?"

"She's the prime suspect in a criminal investigation. We've already subpoenaed her phone records, her bank records and gotten a search warrant for her house. What we haven't done is had the two of you sit down and talk things out. I'm going to contact Wren and see if we can set up a meeting."

"Now?"

"I want this over with, and I know you do, too. The sooner, the better." He pulled out his phone, sent a quick text.

"I told Wren I wanted to meet with Mary Alice. She wasn't agreeable to the idea," Honor said, but for the first time in days, she felt hopeful that they'd be able to get some answers.

"We keep hitting roadblocks and dead ends,

we all know that Mary Alice is the key to a breakthrough, so I have a feeling Wren will be open to the idea now."

"I'm sure the team is anxious to close this case. We're wasting a lot of manpower on it."

"It has nothing to do with wasting manpower. Wren is concerned for your well-being. I'm just as concerned. Maybe more so." He reached past her and turned off the gas burner, and she realized the kettle had been whistling.

She also realized how close he was, and how much she wanted to step into his arms again.

She stepped back, bumping into the oven.

"This isn't working," she muttered.

"What?"

"The two of us in the kitchen together," she replied.

"I was thinking it was working really nicely," he responded.

"Radley, I don't know what your game is, but you should probably stop. I'm not the kind of person that falls in love easily. I've never been one of those girly-girls chasing after her next happily-ever-after. I've always been content to do my own thing and go my own way, and I don't want to fall for someone who isn't interested in falling for me." The words escaped in a rush, and she could feel heat shooting up her neck and across her cheeks.

"Who said I wasn't interested in falling?" he asked.

"I..." For maybe only the second time in her life, she was speechless.

"You look surprised."

"I am."

"Why?"

"Because I'm me and you're you, and we work together. It could be awkward."

"I've thought about that," he said, still so close she could see the fine lines near his eyes and the flecks of silver in them.

"And?"

"I don't see why it should be a problem. We established at the beginning of all this that we barely speak to each other at work."

"And, we established that we were fine with that."

"Actually," he said, leaning even closer, his warm breath fanning her lips. "If I remember correctly, I was wondering why we didn't talk more and thinking that maybe we should have."

"What does that have to do with anything?"

"Did I ever mention that I almost got married once upon a time?"

"I don't think we've had much of a chance to talk about personal things," she hedged, her mouth dry, her fingers itching to touch his face, feel the rough stubble on his jaw.

"I was young. Early twenties. Still in the military. My fiancée thought I was too committed to my work and not committed enough to her. She told me I needed to choose between one and the other."

"I'm sorry, Radley," she said, imagining how it must have felt to be him—in love but still longing to make a difference in the world, still wanting to pursue his passions and goals.

"I'm not. It helped me see that my work was important, that I felt more fulfilled in it than I did in that relationship. It kept me from making a mistake I'd have regretted eventually. And, if you think about it long enough, you might even say it brought me here. To you."

"I might?"

"Sure," he said, smiling into her eyes.

And, she was caught there, breathless and hopeful, a dozen dreams she'd never allowed herself filling her mind. A house. A puppy. A white picket fence. Children. Christmases. Laughter. Love.

"If you think about it long enough," he murmured against her lips.

And she didn't pull away.

She didn't tell him to stop.

She let herself sink into the sweetness of the moment with him.

He got lost in the moment, in the addictive taste of her lips, the warmth of her breath against his. The whisper-soft touch of her hands as they flitted from his waist to his nape.

His cell phone rang, and he wanted to ignore it, wanted to stay right where he was. In her arms.

But a killer was still on the loose, and Radley was waiting to hear from Wren.

He pulled away reluctantly. One hand cupping Honor's cheek, the other reaching for his phone. He was staring into her eyes, and he didn't stop as he answered.

"Hello?" he nearly barked, his voice gruff with longing.

"No need to be testy, Radley. You're the one who texted me," Wren said, a hint of amusement in her voice.

"Sorry, I was—"

"I'm assuming you're with Honor since you texted me about setting up a meeting." She cut him off.

"Right."

"For the record, there's no hard-and-fast rule

about office relationships. As long as you're not out on the field together—which you won't be—I don't see it as a problem."

He wasn't one to blush. Ever. But his cheeks heated.

"For the record," he responded, still watching Honor. Her lips were pink from his kiss, her eyes the deep blue of the sky at twilight, "I'd transfer if I needed to."

"Noted, but I didn't call to discuss your budding relationship."

"Why do you think we have a—?"

"I called because you suggested setting up a meeting between Honor and Mary Alice. Let's go ahead and do it," she cut him off, not allowing him to deny what they both knew was true.

"Now?" he asked, surprised at how quickly she wanted to move on it.

"Ms. Stevenson is very controlled, very focused and very careful. Having her escorted to our offices in the early hours of the morning might shake her up just enough to get the truth out of her. I, for one, am more than ready to hear it. If Honor is up for it, let's get it done."

"Are you willing to have the meeting now?" he asked Honor, and she nodded.

"There's no time like the present," she responded. "I'll get dressed."

She nearly the ran from the room, and he

knew she was fleeing from him and what they'd shared.

He almost followed, but she needed time, and he had a job to do. He needed to get her to the field office, make certain that she had the meeting with Mary Alice.

This might be the answer they were looking for, an end to the weeks of uncertainty and fear for Honor's safety.

He woke Jessica, filled her in on the plan, grabbed his coat and waited at the door. Minutes later, Honor appeared at the top of the stairs. Dressed in faded jeans and a fitted sweater, hair pulled into a high ponytail, she looked casual, natural and beautiful in a way he couldn't remember any other woman ever being.

He took her coat from the closet and helped her into it, his fingers skimming her nape as he lifted the end of her ponytail from her collar.

"Thanks," she murmured, her cheeks pink.

"No problem," he said, then leaned in and whispered in her ear. "We'll talk later."

"About?" she whispered back, her gaze darting to Jessica.

"Would you like me to go into details?" he asked, and she shook her head, laughing nervously.

"That's okay. I've got a pretty good imagination. I'll figure it out."

"Secrets are only fun for the people who are whispering them to each other," Jessica said, opening the door and stepping outside. "So, how about you two stop with the sweet nothings murmured into each other's ears and start acting like we've got a job to do?"

"We weren't whispering sweet nothings," Honor protested, her cheeks scarlet.

"Of course you weren't," Jessica said, a wry edge to her voice. "And, I'm not grumpy when people wake me up before dawn. Come on. Let's get going."

"Right. Sorry," Honor said, hurrying outside after her.

Radley followed, anxious to get to Boston, to listen to what Mary Alice had to say. He was hoping she'd open up to her friend in a way she'd refused to open up to law enforcement.

If not, they'd be back at square one.

The drive to Boston was uneventful, the conversation easy. Honor seemed relaxed, and he was happy to see her that way. After weeks of tension and fear, she seemed…content.

By the time they arrived at the field office, Mary Alice was sitting at a small desk in an interrogation room. She stood as they entered, her face pale, her hair hanging around her gaunt face.

"This is an odd time for a meeting," she said quietly. "But I'm glad it's finally happening."

"Me too." Honor said, glancing at the two-way mirror on the wall across from them. She knew, of course, that they were being observed and listened to. He wasn't sure if Mary Alice did.

"I've missed you," Honor continued.

"I've missed you, too," Mary Alice said, her voice breaking.

"It didn't seem that way when you were avoiding my phone calls, text messages and emails. So how about we both have a seat, and we can talk about what you were thinking when you went no-contact with a friendship that we've shared for over two decades."

Mary Alice glanced at Radley. "I'd rather talk to you alone."

"You're going to be disappointed then." There was no hint of sympathy in Honor's voice, no hint of softness. That surprised him.

It must have surprised Mary Alice, too.

She straightened, her eyes flashing with irritation. "I'm not the one who called this meeting, Honor. So, how about we do things my way? Otherwise, I may decide it was a bad idea and leave."

"I don't think you'd do that."

"You're underestimating me."

"Or overestimating our friendship."

At her words, Mary Alice's bravado dropped away. "You mean the world to me, Honor. You know that."

"I knew that. Now I'm not so sure. Someone is trying to kill me. You're my best friend. I'd think you'd want to do everything in your power to keep that from happening."

"You know I do."

"Then Tumberg is staying, and there are other agents listening in." She gestured to the mirror. "That's what happens when you lie to law enforcement officials. They start getting suspicious and wondering what you have to hide."

"I didn't lie about anything." Mary Alice dropped into a chair, and Honor did the same.

"You didn't tell the truth," she pointed out.

"Because… I couldn't. I can't." She sighed.

"Why not?"

"I did something really stupid, and now I'm suffering the consequences."

"How stupid and what consequences?" Honor asked, as cold and detached as Radley had ever seen her. She might spend most of her time working on computers, but she knew how to conduct an interview. Even with someone she obviously cared about.

"Honor," Mary Alice swallowed hard, tears

suddenly streaming down her face. "I'm pregnant, and I know what you're going to think about that. I know how disappointed you're going to be."

Honor reached across the table, held Mary Alice's hand, looked into her eyes. "This is the secret? The thing that was keeping you from telling law enforcement the truth about how you ended up at The Sanctuary? You're pregnant?"

"Not all of it." She was still crying, and Radley grabbed a box of tissues from the end of the table and handed it to her.

"Thanks," she mumbled, dabbing at her eyes, still clutching Honor's hand. "There's more, and it's the worst part."

"Is the baby's father Scott?" Honor asked, a hint of disgust in her voice.

Mary Alice shook her head.

"Someone at work?"

"No."

"Come on, Mary Alice. It's too early in the morning for this. We're all exhausted, and I'm not in the mood to play twenty questions. If there's some reason why you don't feel like you can tell me, I'll be glad to go back home and—"

"It's Bennett."

"Who's Bennett?" Honor asked, her brow

furrowed, because, of course, those things wouldn't correlate in her brain. Her best friend and her uncle. A baby.

But they were correlating in Radley's, all the pieces of the puzzle clicking into place.

"The baby's father is Bennett," Mary Alice responded, swiping at her tears and pushing away from the table. She paced across the room and back again, still lean as a whip, no hint of a baby bump. "And I know it was stupid. I know he's a player, a liar and a cheat, but he made me feel good after what happened with Scott."

"You are telling me," Honor said, clearly enunciating ever word, "that you and Bennett were together? That you, for whatever reason, decided it would be smart to get into a relationship with a man who's twenty years your senior, and—"

"Honor," Radley warned, placing a hand on her shoulder, because the emotions she'd done a great job of hiding were bubbling to the surface.

"I'm not finished," she replied, and he glanced at the two-way mirror, wondering when Wren was going to call a halt to things.

"You had a relationship with my uncle. You got pregnant. I'm assuming one of you broke things off," she continued, and Mary Alice nodded.

"I did. There were some things he was doing

that I didn't like. That's what I wanted to talk to you about, but I can see you're upset. I understand why. I really do. This is a huge betrayal of trust, and I'm sorry, Honor. I'll understand if you never want to speak to me again." She was sobbing now, her shoulders shaking, her arms crossed over her stomach.

Radley wasn't one to be overly sympathetic about people's mistakes, but he couldn't deny feeling sorry for her. He'd met Bennett, and he had a feeling the lawyer could manipulate anyone into doing just about anything.

"First, I would never not speak to you again," Honor said, quietly. "I love you, and we're going to get through this. But someone wants me dead, and the police think you have something to do with it. I don't want my... cousin?—" she frowned "—being born in prison. So sit down, and let's start from the beginning."

Mary Alice dropped into the chair again. "The beginning was the day I found out Scott was cheating. I thought we'd have forever together, and when I realized I was wrong, I felt lost."

"And I guess my uncle was there to help you find your way back home?" Honor asked. To her credit, she kept any hint of sarcasm out of her voice.

"He was representing one of the guys I worked with in a DWI case. He came to the office a few times, and eventually he asked me if I'd like to have dinner. I said yes. It was something to do, and I thought we were having fun."

"Until?"

"He asked for money a couple of times. Ten thousand once. Five thousand another time. He said he was waiting on some retainers to clear and had to pay some bills."

"Did you lend him the money?" Radley asked, curious as to why a high-profile lawyer would be low on funds.

"Of course not. I was really turned off by it. We'd only been going out for a couple of months, and I started wondering if he just wanted me for my money." She shrugged.

"Is that when you broke up with him?" Honor asked.

"Stupidly, I stayed with him for another couple of months. I found out I was pregnant, and I went over to his condo one night to break the news. We had a nice dinner, and I told him I was having a baby. He didn't seem as upset as I thought he'd be. I was hoping everything was going to work out. But he had to take a phone call, and I walked into his bedroom and saw some papers sitting on his desk. I wasn't trying to see what they were, but the name on the top caught my eye, so I looked. Honor, he'd had papers drawn up to sell your grandmother's property. I'm not sure if he planned to forge her signature or to trick her into signing them."

"What?" Honor jumped to her feet. "Why didn't you tell me?"

"He came into the room and saw me with them, and he told me that he wanted to make a good life for me and the baby, and that selling your grandmother's farm would give us a fresh start in a new place. He said that a developer wanted the land and was willing to pay ten million dollars for it."

"That is a lot of money," Honor said, her face leached of color, the story obviously impacting her more than she wanted to show.

"It is, and he said that it would help you and Dotty, too. But I know Dotty, and I know she wouldn't sell for any amount of money. I told him that, and he lost it. He started screaming about how it was his farm, and that his mother planned to hand it off to you, and that the only way he would ever get what he was due was to force Dotty to sell. He said the settlement date was a month away, and if I messed it up, he'd take everyone he loved from me. You. My parents. The baby."

"Honey," Honor said, reaching for her hand again. "You had to know I wouldn't let that happen."

"I would have come to you, Honor, but I was at work the next day, and he sent me an email. It was a picture of my parents sleeping, and a note that said he knew plenty of men who could do his dirty work for me. He included the contact information for Sunrise Spiritual Sanctuary, and he told me that I'd better disappear until the real estate deal was done, or my mother would be the first to die."

"We checked your phone records," Radley reminded her. "There's no record of those texts or calls."

"Because Bennett insisted we use disposable phones. If you don't believe me, you can check the room I was staying in at the training center. I left my phone on the top shelf of the closet there. I was tired of the games, and I just wanted it to be over."

"I believe you," Honor said quietly, her fingers tapping on the tabletop. "Did you give Bennett my room number?"

"Not intentionally. He showed up at the training center and told me you'd been hospitalized. He said I should call and make sure you were okay, so I did. He was standing next to me when I wrote down your room number."

"And he passed it along to Absalom." Radley turned to the door and wasn't surprised to find Wren and Henry standing there.

"You're not going maverick on us, Radley," Wren said. "This guy is dangerous, and he's cunning. From what I've heard, he decided that the best way to make certain his deal went off without a hitch was to get Honor out of the way."

"He knew I'd protest a sale. He could probably forge papers giving himself power of attorney, but he would never have convinced me that Dotty had agreed to sell. I'd have fought it, and he'd have been caught," Honor said, still sitting at the table, still tapping her fingers against the wood. "I should have figured this out before now. I think I recognized his voice when he pushed me in the well. I guess my mind just didn't want to accept it."

"It's hard to think someone we love would harm us," Wren said.

"This is my fault," Mary Alice cut in. "I should never have gone out to dinner with him. You used to tell me what a womanizer he was. You used to say that the number of women he wined and dined made you sick."

"He's a charming manipulator, and he used you," Honor responded. "He is totally and wholly responsible for what he's done, and I'm going to make sure he pays for it."

She was up like a shot, racing past Radley, darting out the door. Running for the exit. Radley knew exactly where she planned to go. Bennett's place.

He ran after her, because as much as he wanted justice done, he couldn't let her be the one to mete it out.

THIRTEEN

Meeting her uncle at the farm was the last thing Honor had planned to do.

Then again, she hadn't had a plan when she'd raced from the field office and tried to hail a cab.

Radley had stopped her, pulling her away from the curb, his grip gentle but unyielding. He must have known how enraged she was, how far beyond reason she'd been pushed.

She'd never seen red before, but she was seeing it then, everything cast in the hazy crimson glow of her rage.

Bennett had used Mary Alice, gotten her pregnant, threatened her. He'd been plotting to steal Dotty's farm, take the money from the sale and leave town. Maybe leave the country.

And he'd been trying to kill Honor.

That, oddly, hadn't been the hot-button issue.

It had been what he'd done to Mary Alice—

turning a woman of high moral standards into someone who was scared, ashamed and guilt-ridden—that had made her want to do him bodily harm.

But Radley had stopped her.

They'd gone back to the interview room. They'd finished taking Mary Alice's statement, they'd dug around in Bennett's previous criminal cases and discovered that he'd gotten Absalom off on serious drug charges four years ago, and that he'd done it pro bono.

That was the connection they'd been looking for, and they had a decent case against her uncle.

A confession would be better.

A confession would assure that he went jail and never again saw the light of day.

Honor knew it.

When Wren had mentioned that the evidence was circumstantial, Honor had volunteered to try to get what they needed.

Radley had been dead set against it. He'd wanted to arrest Bennett immediately, but Wren had pointed out that an attorney of his caliber and connections would be out on bail before the sun set, and probably out of the country before it rose again.

Until Bennett was in jail, Mary Alice wouldn't be safe.

Dotty wouldn't be safe.

And the baby—that tiny little innocent life that was so unexpected, so surprising—it wouldn't be safe either.

Because, Bennett had no conscience, and someone like that would do anything to keep his secrets.

Even murder his own child.

Honor had explained that to Radley. She'd told him that she wouldn't sleep until she could rest in the knowledge that her uncle was locked away for good.

Instead of arguing, he'd touched her face, let his palm rest against her cheek. He'd looked into her eyes, and he'd told her that he understood, he stood behind her, he'd do whatever he could to help.

And, right then and there, she'd fallen just a little harder and a little deeper for him.

Now she was sitting on the old porch swing, watching the sunset, waiting for her uncle to show up. No gun, because he'd notice that. She *was* wearing a wire, and FBI agents were stationed around the property, hidden from view, but waiting to move in if they were needed.

She hoped they wouldn't be needed.

Now that her anger had faded, she didn't want Bennett hurt. He was Dotty's oldest son, and if something happened to him, she'd be heartbroken.

What Honor wanted was for Bennett to be arrested, to face a jury of his peers and be found guilty of attempted murder. She wanted him to spend the rest of his life in jail, far away from the people he'd tried to hurt.

She'd called him a few hours ago, told him that she'd spoken to Mary Alice, that she knew about the sale of the farm, and that she wanted to discuss it with him. In the story she'd told, she was strapped for cash, tired of commuting back and forth on the weekends, sick of the dirt and the hay and the endless acres of crops. If he was going to sell the farm, she wanted in on the deal. They could use part of the proceeds to find a good *home* for Dotty, and the rest they'd split.

The lies hadn't come easily. Fortunately, he hadn't been able to see her face. She was certain her expression would have given her away. As it was, by the end of the conversation, he'd agreed to meet with her, and he'd promised to bring the contract and sale agreement.

With Dotty and Mary Alice safe in her apartment in Boston, Honor had no concern that they'd be harmed. All she had to do was keep her cool, get a confession and step back as the arrest was made.

Easy-peasy, as Dotty liked to say.

Only Bennett was supposed to arrive at five-thirty and he still hadn't shown by six. She didn't dare speak into the microphone or try to contact any of the agents who were stationed around the property. Bennett wasn't stupid. It was possible he'd parked his car far from the house and had walked onto the property.

She waited another half hour, the sky darkening, the moon sliding above the trees. Stars glittered against the violet sky, and he still hadn't shown. She'd wrapped herself in a shawl when she'd come out to the porch, but she needed a coat.

She glanced at the driveway. Still no sign of Bennett's car.

Wren had warned her to stay on the porch where they could see her, but her teeth were chattering, and the coat closet was a foot from the front door. She wouldn't even have to step inside.

She stood, stretching a kink out of her back as she opened the front door.

Bennett was there. A shadowy figure in the darkness, but she knew him.

"Uncle Bennett!" she nearly screamed. "How did you get in here?"

"I have a key, remember?" He grabbed her arm, yanked her inside and slammed the door.

"But I didn't see you drive up," she hedged, her heart hammering so loudly she thought he might be able to hear it.

"I parked on the highway at the back edge of the property and walked in."

"Why would you do something like that?"

"Because I don't trust you, Honor. Why else?"

"I'm not the one who tried to commit murder," she responded. "If anyone should be untrusting, it should be me."

"That's exactly right, my dear. You shouldn't trust me, and yet, you asked me out here. Why?"

"I told you on the phone—"

He shoved her up against the wall, his hand against her throat, the attack so sudden and unexpected that she had no time to protect herself.

"You're trying to set me up," he growled, his grip so tight that she couldn't breathe.

She shook her head, frantically clawing at his fingers, trying to loosen his grip.

"You are! Tell me where they're hiding. Tell me what they know!" he screamed, his grip loosening just enough for her to breathe.

"I don't know what you're talking about," she said, the last word ending on a raspy cough.

"Don't lie to me, Honor. You've never been

good at it. It's a shame, because you're mouthy enough to have made a good lawyer." His hand dropped away, and he stepped back.

She expected help to come running, but it didn't. No frantic pounding of fist on the door. No glass shattering as agents breached the house.

They knew what was happening.

She had to assume they were giving her time to get what she'd come for.

So, she had to get her head back in the game and try.

"I'm better at it than you think, Uncle Bennett. Look at Dotty. I have her convinced I love coming out here to help with the farm." She tried to shrug nonchalantly. She wasn't sure how convincing it was. "She thinks I want to take over one day, but I'm just biding my time until she dies. I know she's willed the place to me."

"How did you find out?" he asked, his eyes still hot with anger.

"She told me. She even showed me the will."

"You could have made this easy on both of us and killed her," he spat, still watching her closely. Still not believing her story.

She knew that, but she didn't know what answer he expected her to give, so she went with the truth. "I may be greedy, but I'm not a murderer. You, on the other hand, don't seem to have any qualms."

"What are you accusing me of, Honor?" he said quietly, and she was reminded of a serpent's hiss right before it struck.

"I'm not accusing you of anything. I'm stating a fact. You've been trying to get me out of the way. You're fortunate I'm as eager to get the money as you are, or I'd have turned you in to Wren the minute Mary Alice told me about the property sale."

He didn't just hiss like a snake, he struck like one, his fist slamming into her side with so much force she felt a rib crack. Her eyes teared with pain, and she bent over, trying to catch her breath, to think of where to go from here.

"Where are they?" he growled, dragging her head up by the ponytail, backhanding her so hard she tasted blood.

"If my friends," she managed to say with more strength than she felt, "were standing around waiting for information while you beat me up, I'd need a whole new group of friends."

He scowled, but released her hair, stepping back and pulling a sheaf of papers from his jacket pocket. "This," he said, "is the contract. I need Dotty's signature. The Realtor who wrote up the papers isn't crooked, and he's going to want verification that she's willing to sell. The settlement day is the thirtieth, and he's coming to the house."

"And you want me to convince her to sign away the house and the land?"

"For ten million dollars, that old bat should be willing to sign away her life," he replied.

"She's your mother," she reminded him without thinking.

"No. She's not. She's your father's mother. I'm the product of an affair my father had at the beginning of their marriage. A little indiscretion. Neither of them ever told me, but I always wondered why I was so different from your father. Not just my looks. Everything. The way I thought and felt. What I wanted. We were diametrically opposed, the two of us. The good brother and the evil one, if you want." He grinned.

"If they didn't tell you, you can't be sure."

"Of course I can. Dotty keeps a record of everything. My adoption paperwork is in her file cabinet. I met my birth mother when I was eighteen. She was on her third marriage by then. Not that any of it matters. Except for this part. I am the oldest son, and this land belongs to me. Dotty is only leaving it to you because I'm not her biological son."

"Uncle Bennett! You know that's not true! Dotty loves you."

"People love ice cream, Honor. They love sunrises and movies and good books. They love pretty days and pets and a million things that mean nothing. Love is a construct created by people so that they can feel good about their world. I turned my back on the idea a long time ago. What I want is freedom, and you know how a person gets that?"

"Money?" she guessed, sidling away, trying to put some space between them. She wanted the confession, but she wanted to live, too. Unlike Bennett, she didn't believe love was a human construct. It was a God-given emotion and a divine directive. She believed in it with every fiber of her being, and if he'd known anything about her, he'd have known that love would prevent her from ever betraying Dotty.

He didn't, though, and he still had the contract in hand, and was waving it toward her. "That's right. Money. After taxes, I stand to clear enough money from the sale of this farm to live in luxury for the rest of my life."

"A million dollars isn't as much as it used to be, Uncle Bennett, and the rest of your life could be a very long time."

"Not here, Honor," he laughed without humor. "Thailand or Mexico. Somewhere my dollar stretches."

"Your dollar should stretch far here if you

were good with your money. Personally, I don't understand how a lawyer who charges as much as you do can be so desperate for cash that he'd try to kill someone to pad his pockets."

He lunged at her, but this time she sidestepped, kicking his feet out from under him and watching dispassionately as he fell. At least, that was the look she was going for. She felt physically ill at the thought of his greed, of the evil that he hid behind his cold smiles and gracious manners.

He came up with a gun in his hand, the barrel pointed at her heart. "If you do that again, niece, I will kill you without a qualm. I'll make it look like a robbery gone wrong. I'll comfort my poor grieving mother, and then I'll put the pen in her hand and watch while she signs the farm away."

"If you thought you could get away with it, you'd have already killed me," she said, walking down the hall and into the kitchen, her heart pounding frantically. There were more windows there. The back door. She had no idea where Radley was, where Wren had gone, what Henry or Jessica were doing, but she had to believe that they'd know when the time was right, and that they'd step in before it was too late.

"You're right. I know enough about the way

things work to know how difficult it is to commit the perfect crime. That's why I prefer that other people do my dirty work," he said, following her into the kitchen. There was a knife block on the counter, a broom in the corner. She could see several items she could use as a weapon. None of them would be effective against a gun.

"That's why you did the work for Absalom pro bono, right? You figured you might be able to call in the favor one day."

"What do you know about that?" he said quietly, his tone chillingly still.

"Just what I found out in my research. You see, Uncle, you're not the only one who likes to control things. I've learned a lot from watching you, and I don't believe in leaving things to chance," she said, finally getting to the script she'd worked out with the team. The one that should lead him into the confession.

"What's that supposed to mean?"

"I did my research before contacting you. I know you sent Mary Alice to The Sanctuary and paid Absalom to keep her there. I know that you told her she needed to stay until after the farm was sold. I also know that my traveling to The Sanctuary was part of your plan from the very beginning. You wanted me somewhere far away from work, where an accident could happen, and I could die. Only there were a lot more people in The Sanctuary than you realized, and Absalom had to improvise. First, drug my food. Then, push me into a clay-firing pit. The next step was easy. Just let me die of natural causes. Infection. Fever. Dehydration. Whatever took me first. It was a good plan, but not the perfect crime you were hoping for. Knowing I'd survived must have been a difficult pill to swallow, considering how much you hate losing." She smiled, purposely goading him.

And he took the bait, the gun dropping a fraction as he stepped toward her, his eyes blazing. "You want to know the truth, Honor? You've always been in the way. I never wanted to be your guardian. I agreed to do it because I knew if your parents died, I'd have access to the money they were going to leave you. You were too young to realize how much there was, and later, you were too stupid to ask me for an accounting of it. I guess that was fortunate for you, because if you had, you'd have been dead a long time ago."

"It's nice to know how much you cared, Uncle Bennett. So, now let's discuss the deal. You get a quarter of the sale. I get the rest."

"What?"

"I put all that information together, everything I just told you. I have it in a safety deposit box, and I left a note in my work desk. If you kill me, my boss will find it, and you'll go to jail. If you refuse my offer, I'll go to my boss, and you'll go to jail. Either way, you lose. I guess that's what happens when you underestimate the person you try to have killed."

"I should have done the job myself while you were at The Sanctuary," he growled, lifting the gun again, pointing it straight at her head. "If I hadn't hired that idiot Absalom, you'd be dead. But I can remedy the situation easily enough."

She dropped to the ground, knowing he'd pull the trigger, frantic to escape. Rolling toward the hall as glass shattered and the gun exploded. She expected the impact of the bullet, braced herself for it, but Bennett was on the ground beside her, blood pouring from his chest, his eyes blazing with hatred.

"You set me up," he howled, somehow springing up and over her, hands around her throat, and she was fighting for her life as the back door frame splintered and the world turned to chaos.

Radley dragged Bennett up and away from Honor, swinging the guy with so much force he flew across the room. Bennett slammed into the counter, sagged onto the ground, then was up again, reaching for the block of knives.

Radley had his body covering Honor's, his gun in hand. He aimed at Bennett's hand.

"Don't do it, Bennet!" he shouted.

"You never betray family," Bennett replied, his eyes wild, blood seeping from the wound in his chest. "Never!"

"Freeze!" Wren yelled as she entered the kitchen, her gun drawn, pointed, ready.

Bennett had the knife in his hand now, and he swung toward her.

Wren took the shot, and he was down, chaos to calm. Motion to stillness. All of it in just the beat of a heart. Nothing but the quiet drip of the kitchen faucet and Honor's hitched breathing, the soft rustle of Wren's clothes as she moved across the room and checked Bennet's pulse.

He was dead.

Radley knew it, and he lifted Honor, turning so that she couldn't see her uncle, carrying her through the hall and outside.

He kept going until they reached the edge of the yard, and he set her on the cool aromatic grass, sitting beside her, pulling her close, wiping away the tears that were sliding down her cheeks.

"I'm sorry," he said quietly, kissing her forehead, her cheeks, her lips. Wishing he could offer her more than words.

"Me too," she responded, sliding her arm around his waist and resting her head on his shoulder. "A family destroyed. All because of money."

"He wasn't family, Honor. Dotty is. Mary Alice. The baby she's going to have. They're family. Wren, Henry, Jessica. The Special Crimes Unit. That's family. People who stand beside you, who support you, who will sacrifice anything for you. That is family."

"You didn't include yourself," she said, and he shifted so that they were facing each other, so that he could look into her tearstained face, into her beautiful eyes.

"Because I want to be more than family," he replied, brushing another tear from her cheek and letting his palm rest against her velvety skin. "I love you, Honor. And I want to be the epic hero you don't need. The one who knows just how strong and capable you are, but who is always just a few steps away. Waiting. Just in case. I want to be the happily-ever-after you weren't looking for, the place you always want to return."

"Home?" she said. "Because that's where I am when I'm with you. I love you, Radley. I want you to know that, because life is short, and things happen, and I don't want to ever regret what hasn't been said."

He looked in her eyes, and he saw the truth. The love that had surprised them both, the gift that neither had asked for but that God had granted.

"Home," he agreed as he kissed her again, and then they sat on the cool grass, watching as the moon rose in the sleepy night sky and the ambulance arrived to carry Bennett away.

EPILOGUE

So this was what it was like to walk into forever.

Flowers in the hair. Fancy white dress. Snow falling outside the chapel windows.

Knees shaking.

Stomach churning.

Hands trembling.

And, Honor, standing like a ninny with tears in her eyes, because what she'd never dared hope for was about to happen.

Her father wasn't there to give her away.

Her mother wasn't there to see it.

Her uncle, if he had lived, wouldn't have been worthy to do either of those things.

But Dotty was to her left, Mary Alice to her right, her church family and friends waiting on the other side of the double doors that led into the sanctuary.

And it was good.

All of it.

Beautiful and right.

Soon the doors would open, and she'd walk the few-dozen feet to Radley's side. She'd look into his eyes and speak the vows that would bind them together through a lifetime of joys and challenges.

And, they would make it last.

She knew they would, because they had what her parents had once demonstrated—friendship, laughter, respect. All of it bound together with love.

She took a deep breath, inhaling joy. Exhaling nerves.

"No sniffling and ruining that beautiful makeup," Dotty whispered loudly as organ music drifted into the vestibule. Dressed in a powder-blue dress, her hair curled, she looked stronger than she had since Bennett's funeral.

Maybe, like Honor, she felt a sense of renewal and vigor, a returning of hope and joy.

"I never cry," Honor said.

"Humph," Mary Alice responded, tucking her arm through Honor's because the music was swelling, the bridal march about to begin.

"What?" Honor demanded, meeting her friend's eyes, wishing she could wash away the guilt and shame she saw each time she looked in them.

"You cried last month. When we had the

sonogram and found out I'm having a girl." Mary Alice touched her stomach, the gesture unconsciously protective.

She loved the little girl she was carrying. There was no doubt about that, but there was a sadness to her now that had never been there before. She'd returned to her job a few months ago, throwing herself into work the way she once had. Her parents had embraced and encouraged her effort to move forward with life. But Mary Alice had changed, her joyful, carefree personality replaced by a cautious, careful approach to life. Now, nearly nine months pregnant, she was preparing for motherhood with a quiet happiness that seemed, sometimes, overshadowed by her guilt.

"I cried because you told me you were naming the baby after our mothers. If joy isn't a good reason to cry, I don't know what is," Honor responded, hoping to make her friend smile.

"Today is one of the most joyful days of my life, and tears are totally appropriate for both of us," Mary Alice said solemnly, tears shimmering in her eyes. "You are stunning, Honor, and I'm so happy for you. Of all the people I know and love, you are the one most deserving of happily-ever-after."

"You are deserving, too, and one day, it will

happen. When you least expect it and aren't looking for it. When you think every chance is gone and you are content with what you have, suddenly God will send just the right person into your life," Honor said, hugging Mary Alice close, fabric rustling, the baby bump between them.

"He already did," Mary Alice said, touching her stomach again.

"Girls, enough of this talk. We'll all be crying soon, and a woman my age can't afford to have a tear-stained face," Dotty chided, her voice rough with emotion.

"Right. No tears," Mary Alice said with a wide grin that reminded Honor of long-ago days when they'd been young and carefree and filled with happiness.

It gave her hope for her friend.

The music reached a crescendo and the doors swung open, the sanctuary glimmering in the soft light of a hundred candles.

She could see Radley, standing at the front of the church, his eyes gleaming with love and happiness. And her soul seemed to reach for his, acknowledging the sacredness of the moment and of what they would soon share.

She took the first step and the next, Dotty and Mary Alice beside her. When she finally reached his side, Radley took her hand, and her heart swelled with a love so real and deep it took her breath away.

"I love you," he said, his hushed words ringing through the now-quiet sanctuary.

"I love you," she replied. "Forever and always."

She heard Dotty sniffle, saw Mary Alice brush a tear away, and then the pastor was speaking, the ceremony beginning, the future stretching out as bright and beautiful as a summer sunrise.

And the lifetime of love she'd never dared hope for came true.

* * * * *

If you enjoyed this story,
don't miss the previous books in the
FBI: Special Crimes Unit series
from Shirlee McCoy:

Night Stalker
Gone

And be sure to pick up these other exciting
books by Shirlee McCoy:

Protective Instincts
Her Christmas Guardian
Exit Strategy
Deadly Christmas Secrets
Mystery Child
The Christmas Target
Mistaken Identity
Christmas on the Run

Available now from Love Inspired Suspense!

Find more great reads at
www.LoveInspired.com

Dear Reader,

Love is a word we use often. We love cars and movies, books and food. Of course, we love people, too. Spouses, children, family and friends. They all fall in the category of things we enjoy. But love is so much deeper than that. Love isn't just the quick happy feeling we get when we share an experience with someone we care about. It is not the attraction we feel when we look into the eyes of our significant others. It isn't the warmth we feel when we hold our babies for the first time. Love is not warm and fuzzy, sweet and light. It is hard work. It is sacrifice. It is commitment to the betterment of someone else even at the expense of self.

FBI agents Radley Tumberg and Honor Remington know this. They live good lives filled with wonderful people. They enjoy the material things that God has provided, and they aren't looking for more. But when Honor's life is threatened and everything she holds dear is in jeopardy, Radley steps in to help, and the love neither of them is looking for finds them.

I hope you enjoy the third book in the FBI Special Crimes Unit. I love hearing from readers. You can find me on Facebook, Instagram and Twitter, and if you have the time, drop me a line at shirlee@shirleemccoy.com.

Blessings,
Shirlee McCoy